ACTS
BY E-MAIL

The story of a church...
with a twist of lemon

Martha B. Hook

xulon
PRESS

Acts By E-mail
by Martha B. Hook

Printed in the United States of America

Library of Congress Control Number: 2002093395
ISBN 1-591601-49-5

Xulon Press
11350 Random Hills Road
Suite 800
Fairfax, VA 22030
(703) 279-6511
XulonPress.com

To order additional copies, call 1-866-909-BOOK (2665).

Praise for Acts By E-mail

"Read ACTS BY E-MAIL and you will discover the delightfully creative writing of Martha Hook. This book peels back the layers of quaint, small-town living to reveal unexpected psychological and spiritual tensions. It will certainly prompt you to contemplate how life is not always as it appears. Expect to have your own emotions stirred as you watch how the characters come to terms with unusual events.
 —Les Carter, Ph.D., therapist, author, and speaker.

"Fasten your seat belts for a great read. This story is both profound and insightful, and is what good storytelling is all about. I loved finding the twists of lemon in ACTS BY E-MAIL."
 —LetaFae Arnold, M.Ed., M.A., assoc. professor of English, LeTourneau University, ret.

"Having spent thirty-six years as a pastor, I find Martha Hook's story intriguing, yet almost too close for comfort. As we read about daily episodes of pastoral life, Martha gives us a heartwarming glimpse into the glass house of the ministry. For entertaining reading, I can highly recommend ACTS BY E-MAIL.
 —Lewis Abbott, pastor and ministry consultant.

"Martha Hook is a gifted writer and storyteller. With homespun warmth, she makes you smile, wince, gasp, and grow with Rev. Wayne Latimer and the charming people he shepherds. If you're a Mitford enthusiast, be prepared to fall in love with ACTS BY E-MAIL"

—Kathy Peel, author and president of
Family Manager Inc.

Dedication

For my grandchildren:

Joanna

Lincoln

Melanie

Monica

Samuel

Stewart

Each of you has your own unique story in the ongoing Book of Acts, and your own special place in my heart. You always bring me great joy.

I Love You,
Grammy

Acknowlegements

My thanks to my dear friends and family members who have partnered with me in this project. ACTS BY E-MAIL has been written story by story over twenty-five years' time. Thus, many people have read and re-read this book as it has developed. Each person's response has been a great encouragement to me.

People with special, valued suggestions are LetaFae Arnold and her creative writing class at LeTourneau University, Anne Worth, Trudy Richardson, and Kathy Muntean. I've also relied on my family for their comments: my daughters Brenda Morris, Barbara Nelson, Mary McKee, and my cousins, Lillian Tate and Julie Patrick.

This is a work of fiction. No character is meant to represent any real person. However, as in any writer's experience, bits and pieces of my own journey show up in various chapters and characters. I'm blessed to have had a long life full of fascinating adventures and people. I hope ACTS BY E-MAIL is a reflection of my gratitude.

Martha B. Hook
Dallas, TX
2002

Table of Contents

Cast of Characters

Wayne and Trudy Latimer: The Lily of the Valley Community Church's pastor and wife; their children are Cayla & Joshua.

Chuck and Laurie Latimer: Wayne's older brother and wife; he is a medical missionary in Papua New Guinea; their children are Ashley & Kevin.

Vic and Stella Dabney: builder and beautician; their children are Jenny and Darcy.

Jenny Dabney: Dabneys' daughter; her children are Chelsea and Zachary.

Donny Transome: community troublemaker; Jenny's former lover and Chelsea's father.

Frank and Eva Souter: Vic and Stella Dabney's best friends; they own Home Designs Trailer Company.

Rev. and Mrs. Ike Grant: former LOV Church pastor and wife.

Raleigh Lawrence: U.S. Army officer, Jenny's blind date and Zachary's father.

Dee Wight Smith: Raleigh's cousin; guard at Slocum Prison.

Stefan Gentry: local physician and son of Max and Sally Gentry; he is Chuck and Wayne Latimer's close friend.

Bickerz: assistant to L. Arch Fiend.

L. Arch Fiend: himself.

Max and Sally Gentry: surgeon at Riverton General Hospital; their children are Megan and Stefan. He was Lida Sullivan's high school sweetheart.

Lida and Carter Sullivan: Sunday School teachers at the LOV Church; she was Max's Gentry's high school girlfriend.

Jill Sinclair: single high school teacher.

Mr. Austin: elderly grocer who lives near Jill's vacation cottage.

Jeff Rayburn: Mr. Austin's accomplice.

Sam and Nora Loftis: retired couple. He is the Lakeland County sheriff. Their son is Joel.

Joel Loftis: son of Loftises; coach at Little River High School.

Michael: mysterious caller.

Trevor Langley: treasurer of LOV Church.

Ms. Isabella DeMarco: reclusive single woman.

Ron: Isabella DeMarco's summer romance.

Ed and EmmaLu Sparks: friends of Wayne and Trudy.

JoLena and Pearle: lifelong friends and rivals in Little River.

Sally Mix: single sister of Perry Mix; works at grocery store.

Perry Mix: convicted murderer housed at Slocum Prison.

Rosetta Lawrence: Raleigh's mother and Dee Wight's aunt.

Caroline and Will Blackwell: a farming family, and foster parents for Troy, Carrie and Andrella.

Tina: Andrella's addicted birth mother.

Megan Gentry: Stefan Gentry's twin sister and TV anchorwoman.

Ellen Gentry: Stefan Gentry's wife.

Erika: orphaned girl from Germany.

Prologue

Welcome to the community of Little River, a town in the heart of America. It has all the usual requirements for a small city: a town square, local cafés, grocery stores, gas stations, beauty and barber shops, schools, churches, a hospital, movie theaters, fast food places, a dance hall, several bars, a retirement village, and a large prison on the outskirts of town. Our focus will be on one of the town's smaller churches, The Lily of the Valley Community Church.

Be prepared to feel right at home. This could be your town, your neighbors, your church, or your minister. As usual, the members of the Lily of the Valley Church pray in the tough times, and thank God in the good times. There are few easy solutions. In the midst of it all, God somehow accomplishes His purpose.

Pastor Wayne Latimer, the church's newly installed minister, will be your guide through these stories. The members of his new congregation fascinate him, and he welcomes them and their experiences into his heart. He delights in writing down the stories that particularly showcase God at work in their lives.

Through the miracle of e-mail, Pastor Wayne shares some of his favorite stories with his older brother and confidant, Dr. Chuck Latimer, a medical missionary in Papua New Guinea. These brothers have shared a close bond throughout their lives. Dr. Chuck has recently moved his family across the Pacific Ocean to join the staff of South Pacific Mission. Chuck's e-mail address is: LatimerPNG@sopac.org.

We enter the story as Pastor Wayne is settling his family and his well-used computer into their new surroundings....

Lily of the Valley Community Church

11:00

INSTALLATION CEREMONY

HONORING

REV. WAYNE LATIMER

~~~~~~~~~~~~~~~~~~~~~~~~

OPENING PRAYER

PRAISE SONGS AND HYMNS

INSTALLATION

SPECIAL MUSIC BY THE WORSHIP TEAM

SERMON: REV. WAYNE LATIMER

"Thoughts from a Shepherd's Heart"

SOLO: TRUDY LATIMER

Child Care is available in the Day Care Corral

~~~~~~~~~~~~~~~~~~~~

Everyone is invited to stay for lunch on the grounds

Food by the Women's Connection and Lola's Café

$3 optional donation

LatimerPNG@sopac.org

Subject: First Letter

Hi, Chuck and Laurie,

Time flies! It seems like no time since you were here at the family reunion and we were saying our farewells to everyone. Now you two with Kevin and Ashley are half way around the world, and we are just beginning to feel normal in Little River. Never thought I'd be a preacher, and certainly not in my own hometown.

Thanks so much for taking the time to drive all the way over here to be with us for the installation service. It really meant a lot to us to have your gang and Mom and Dad with us for the big occasion. I know it took extra effort on your part since you were in the middle of packing yourselves up to move to the South Pacific. Mom and Dad were totally blessed to have us all together one last time before you jumped off the edge of the world.

A lot has changed around Little River, but a lot is the same. Funny thing, I lost my bearings the other day coming home from visiting a shut-in over by the river. It never occurred to me that I might get lost in Little River! But that gas station the Transome family used to run isn't there by the turn anymore, and I was almost out of the state before I caught on.

We're still unpacking, and Trudy is pretty well exhausted most of the time. Cayla and Joshua are fine. They have already made some new friends. How do they do that? The parsonage is the same, old and drafty, but we'll warm it up.

So here I am . . ."the" minister where we all grew up. My guardian angel must be working overtime to cover my old tracks. I'm always thinking everyone remembers how bad we were as kids. I'm reminded that "where sin abounds, grace does much more abound." That verse gives me a lot of hope!

Actually, The Lily of the Valley Community Church seems to have survived our developmental stages just fine. Now I hope the church can manage to survive this latest stage of mine for the next few years, or for however long we are here.

I'll have to e-mail you more later about these Lily of the Valley/LOV (isn't that a great acrostic?) people. Their stories are all new to me, and I'm a captive audience. I feel like new chapters of the book of Acts are developing right under my nose. Trust me, it's sturdy stuff. Life in the Fast Lane! Not like those totally predictable novels Mom made us read on family trips.

Around here, everyone's life goes along fine, and then it's like a twist or two of lemon is dropped into the mix. I'll e-mail the stories to you as I write them down. Remember, I'm still dreaming of writing that best-seller novel, and these stories are just the warm-up. Some days I think I really am addicted to writing. Stories are so awesome when they are out of real life. You'll have to forgive a bit of poetic license here and there, but you're used to that.

So, how's Papua New Guinea? How are my favorite missionaries? Hopefully, you're over jet lag and the first round of culture shock by now? I know Laurie has put all your "stuff" in place to make you feel at home. She's good at that. How are Kevin and Ashley handling all the new places and faces? Has Kevin found a soccer buddy yet? Be sure and give them a big hug from Uncle Wayne.

Hook up that computer we gave you so we can stay in

touch on a regular basis. I hear it can take 2-3 weeks to get a snail mail letter. So, hurry, pls.

Pray for the LOV Church. This church needs some serious divine intervention with me at the helm........well, Trudy makes up for a lot. We love and miss you guys. We're praying for you all the time. Everyone says, "Hi."

Prayers and stuff,
Wayne.

Send To | **Attachments**

LatimerPNG@sopac.org

Subject: Need Mail

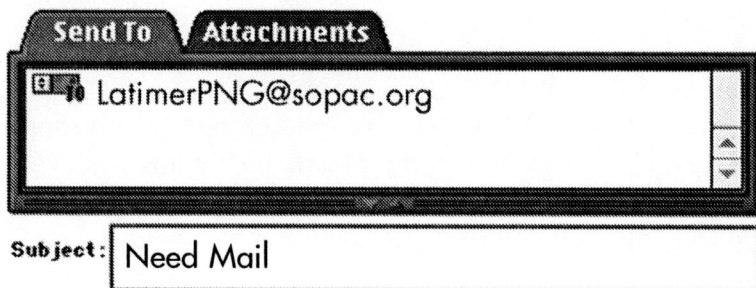

Why aren't you in cyberspace yet? Huh? Huh? At least borrow a computer port and let us know you are alive over there. The Pacific seems double big since we haven't heard squat from you. Holler when you can. I'm serious. The folks are mega-worried.

To entertain myself while I wait for news from your side of the world, I'll send you this story I heard the other day. Remember Vic Dabney, the contractor who built the folks' house? He's working by the hour now. He's sort of slow, but does really beautiful work. He's been patching things up for us here at the parsonage. Trudy's repair list is unending!

The other day I stopped by for a visit over at Dabneys'. Vic and I were having a glass of iced tea while he sneaked a smoke out on the back porch. So I asked him about his family. He gave me an earful about what he and Stella have been through with their daughter, Jenny. You remember she was just a kid when we were in high school? I'll attach Vic's story after this e-mail.

We've been mostly getting the parsonage settled and I've been setting up my office and preparing the next six months of sermons. My outlines from the other church are all new sermons to this new flock, so I'm still loaded with material. Trudy says the same about her wardrobe.

If you have any inspirations for sermons, please e-mail them ASAP. Fair's fair, so do you want any medical insights I may come up with? New uses for rainbow colored bandaids etc.? Also, I'm up for the latest jokes in PNG? Do they know about the chicken crossing the road over there?

Time to go visit Isabelle Demarco. Remember her? Her grandfather died, but she still lives in that old family home. I love to visit and let her go on and on about the Bible. She is one smart lady, and never went to school beyond that women's college years ago. How do you get that smart without studying in the original languages? Maybe that's what I'll ask her about this afternoon…if she makes me a latte.

Ciao,
Wayne

P.S. WRITE/CALL/E-MAIL/SEND CARRIER PIGEON… we'll take anything but a message in a bottle! Well, maybe that would arrive here quicker than anything else, so go ahead….just make it a great bottle that I can sell on e-Bay.

> **Send To** | **Attachments**
>
> Child Care

CHILD CARE

"Daddy, can we go somewhere to talk," Jenny quietly asked her father as they finished clearing the supper dishes.

"Yep, in a minute," Vic replied. Inwardly, he began to brace himself for what might be coming. Jenny usually chattered away about any and everything. Strange request, this one, to talk to him; he suspected that she must have a problem. Maybe she needed money?

When the clean-up was done, and the rest of the Dabney family was settled in to watch TV, Vic and Jenny sat on the sunset side of the house on the back porch. Vic often came out on the porch to smoke after dinner, but it was unusual for someone to join him. No one liked his smoking. Banishment to the porch was supposed to have been his punishment for smoking, but it had evolved into an anticipated time of the day for him. It was sort of "his time."

"Aren't you ever going to quit smoking, Daddy?" asked Jenny.

"Not anytime soon, Sis. Is that what this is all about?" He growled, knowing it probably wasn't. There was a long pause, and finally Vic took Jenny's hand. "What's going on, baby?" he pried.

"Well, Daddy," she said and sniffed. "I'm pregnant again."

"Whooaa," Vic moaned through a cloud of smoke.

Jenny had already had one child, now five year old Chelsea. She'd never married Chelsea's father, Donny Transome. They'd lived together out on the edge of town in

Donny's trailer; but then Donny had been incarcerated on a drug charge.

Even in his childhood, Donny had been "hard to manage." He had been in and out of serious trouble since his early teen years, and was usually at the center of any local fight or disturbance. He always felt like he was treated unfairly by the local police. At his trial he announced that the jury had been rigged. As far as he was concerned, it was simple: everyone was out to get him. He was dominated by a cold sort of rage, but Jenny said he had a "sweet" side to him that other people didn't understand.

She began to have her doubts about him when once he lost his temper over one of infant Chelsea's bad nights. It was clearly a case of colic, and Jenny had done everything she could think of to soothe the baby. Still, Donny was furious and tried to grab Chelsea from her because, "She just needs a good spanking." Jenny had held on to Chelsea, and Donny relented. Now she wondered if she had ever known him at all.

After Donny served some of his time on the drug charges, he was paroled, but he kept breaking appointments with his parole officer. Finally, he started a brawl at one of the seedy bars out on the edge of town, and the judge put him away without even a whisper about any early release. Jenny was 21 the last time the Dabneys had seen anything of Donny Transome.

Jenny had tried to live on her own at the trailer for awhile. But she couldn't keep up Donny's payments, and the trailer was repossessed. In fact, it was almost pulled out from under her and Chelsea. Fortunately, the man from Home Designs Trailer Company, Frank Souter, had known the Dabneys for years, so he waited with his tow truck while Jenny and her mother, Stella, frantically packed up her few belongings.

Vic had told Jenny he would drive her over to Slocum Prison to see Donny, but they never got around to it. This was fine with Vic, who did not think much of Donny Transome and his living arrangements with Jenny. She had not mentioned Donny in awhile. Now, looking back, Vic made some quick mental calculations, and figured the silence started about the time she started romancing someone else.

"I just don't know what to do," she groaned as she held onto Vic's hand. "I'm barely making it now. I think the smartest thing is an abortion. What do you think?"

Now it was Vic's turn to be quiet. He looked deep into the sunset for a long time. Finally, he ground out his cigarette with his boot. Then he put his arms around Jenny and held her like he had when she was Chelsea's age.

"I'm cogitating, sweetheart. Hang on, just hang on a minute," was all he could say. Vic always cogitated when serious issues were at stake.

It was hard for him to keep up with the whirlwind going on in his head. The Dabneys had another daughter, Darcy, to finish rearing. Vic was an hourly construction worker, and Stella ran the beauty shop next to The Lily of the Valley Community Church. It had ruined their budget for them to take Jenny and Chelsea in when Donny's trailer was re-possessed.

But Stella said, "We'll just have to help her, Vic." And Vic had agreed.

"We'll find a way. I'll talk to the foreman at work and see if I can add some extra hours at this new building site they're rushing him on."

"Maybe I can think of something, too," offered Stella. The next week she enrolled in a training course to do sculptured nails. Now all of her friends came in for what they called their "Chelsea Nails."

And Jenny had devised her own plan for survival. She applied to the elders at The Lily of the Valley Community Church with a plan to begin a day care center in the church nursery area. Thus, Day Care Corral was born. It was set up to help working parents in Little River, but it was mostly for Jenny and Chelsea.

The pastor's wife also was interested in the day care center. She was good at organizing the business end of things, and together, she and Jenny built up a friendship and the day care center. The project soon became a full-blown business, and it filled a need in the community. Jenny's self-esteem had grown alongside the success of the Day Care Corral.

At last, Vic spoke softly. "You know, Sis, when you and Chelsea needed help, I told you that this family takes care of its children. Nothing has changed how I feel about that."

"But, Daddy, how can you and Mom take on another of my mistakes? I just feel so awful and so stupid."

"Wait up, Jenny. Children aren't mistakes, our actions maybe, but not the kids. We get ourselves together for better or worse, but only the good Lord can put a baby together. And with all you've done recently at the Day Care Corral, there is lots of evidence that you are far from stupid." He held onto her more tightly. "We'll get through this one, too, Jenny. Now, go find your mother, and let's see what we can figure out."

Stella bustled out, absorbed the news, then asked a lot of questions. They both pried, but Jenny declined to reveal the father's identity. They talked long after the sunset was gone. Finally, neither Stella nor Vic would consider anything but taking care of their own family, including this unborn grandchild. So Jenny took a deep breath and decided to keep her pregnancy.

~~~~~~~~

A few days later, in spite of her parents' support, Jenny's anxiety and misgivings mushroomed and overwhelmed her. She began to consider other options again. Once more she pulled Vic out on the porch after dinner. Chelsea was whining for her mother, but Stella said she'd put her to bed.

"Daddy, I need to talk to you some more about this new baby. I'm beginning to think that an abortion would really be best. I just don't think that I can do this again."

"Now, Jenny, I've already told you what I think. Your mother and I take care of our family, and for now that means you, Chelsea, and this new one. I don't think I could live with myself if I agreed to let you destroy your baby. And you, I'm thinking about you, too. How would you feel about an abortion years from now? Looks to me like it could have a slow burn on your insides."

Jenny nodded, but did not have a reply. Rather feebly, she suggested, "I guess I could put the baby up for adoption? The idea appeals to me, and maybe it would put a happy ending on all this."

Vic went on, "I know adoption is a possibility, but I'm not keen on giving up one of our own if we can all work together to give the child a decent home."

"But, wait a minute. There's something you don't know, Daddy." Jenny was twisting her hands and biting her lip in a way that made Vic nervous. After a long pause she whispered, "This baby is bi-racial. This baby's father is a black man."

Sunset light spread across Vic's face as Jenny searched it for his response. He grimaced, sighed, and looked her straight in the eye.

"Sis, I don't see as how that changes a thing from my point of view. You're still carrying a baby who is going to need a home. It just means a lot of people are going to talk, and we're going to have to love this one a whole bunch. Better yet, love it special."

Jenny leaned her head over on his shoulder and said, "Dad, how did I get so lucky to have you two for parents? I don't know what's the matter with me. I am so lonesome sometimes, and then I start acting crazy-like. The night this happened some of us were just out dancing at Good Times, and afterwards things got out of hand. We all had too much to drink. I'm really sorry, Dad. You and Mom don't deserve this." She snuffled and Vic dug his bandana out of his back pocket for her.

"Well, doesn't this baby's father want to help you? Who in the world is he, anyhow? Anyone I know?

"OK, Daddy, you might as well know. Remember when Donny's old buddy, Jason, fixed me up with his Army friend while Donny was back in prison for messing up his parole? I never told you he was black because I didn't want a big discussion. It was only going to be one date; he was on his way through Little River on leave. We all met at Lola's for dinner and then went out dancing. One thing led to another, and, well, that's it. I've never even heard from the guy since. His name is Raleigh Lawrence."

"Look, I don't care if he's purple, Jenny. In my opinion no man should mix it up with a girl he's just met. I'd sure like to tell this what's his name, Raleigh, a thing or two."

"Me, too. But I decided to let it be. I think it's best to not bring him back into the picture," she paused. "But you know what, Dad? I liked him a lot. He was easy to talk to, great sense of humor, and smart, too. After the first few minutes, I never even thought about his color. At first I was sorry when he didn't stay in touch. Now I hope he stays away. I've definitely changed my opinion of him."

"Right now, I don't think much of this hombre. Hmphf!" growled Vic.

"I don't either, Dad. But remember, this is not just his fault. I am half of this dilemma. I know I'm responsible, too."

Vic winced, then said, " Well, go see if Chelsea has settled down, and let's let your mother ask all her questions about the rest of the story. Brace yourself, Sugar!" he said with a wry grin as he lit another cigarette.

Vic and Stella had been so pleased with how Jenny had

survived Chelsea's arrival. The Day Care Corral was doing so well. Now this. The arrival of a bi-racial baby in their home was something for which they had no precedent; in fact, no one in Little River had faced this scenario before. To use one of Vic's favorite words, they were "bumfuzzled."

After more discussion, the three of them decided to try to make the best home for the baby that they could. The next weekend, Vic started remodeling Chelsea's room to make a corner into a nursery. Jenny then made new curtains, and Stella repainted the old baby bed. And they waited.

~~~~~~

Six months went by, and Jenny's son was born. The Dabneys named him "Zachary." Darcy picked the name, and they all voted on it. The Dabneys always tried for a unanimous vote, and if it wouldn't come, Vic put down the winning vote. This time the vote was unanimous, and Zachary was welcomed into his world with no small fanfare.

Mrs. Ike Grant, the pastor's wife, helped get donations and hand-me-downs for the new arrival. She also made sure that volunteers took over Jenny's job at the Day Care Corral for two weeks. Jenny's friends in the Significant Singles Sunday School class did what they could to help. They stocked the Dabney kitchen with casseroles and goodies, and some just stopped by to be with Jenny and her new infant.

When Jenny returned to her work at the Day Care Corral with Chelsea and Zachary, her life picked up again without much change. Of course, there was an extra child to care for, but except for his ravenous appetite, he was an easy baby.

Chelsea loved her new brother. She soon learned to help with feeding him. "I'm feeding a real baby," she said in a whisper the first time she gave him a bottle.

So Vic's family absorbed this new challenge, and they kept on loving their own. But, the town of Little River was not through with Zachary yet. With his racial characteristics, he was the subject of many discussions. Vic became more and more concerned for Jenny and her well being. He knew about Zachary's father, but few others did, and, in his opinion, they didn't need to know. He even tried to talk with Jenny about quietly letting the truth be known, but she wasn't ready for that.

Jenny's chagrin over having a baby by a man she spent only a few hours with was still a searing pain on her conscience. How she had felt about him on their date hardly seemed relevant at all. It was hard for her to face the future with another baby. But most of all, she wanted to protect herself and her family from what they all knew was inevitable: plain old, hard core gossip.

Finally, she agreed to let Vic talk with their pastor, Ike Grant. And she promised that she would talk with Mrs. Grant. At least two reliable people would know what happened and would be judicious with the facts.

"Why can't people just let Zachary be a normal little guy?" Jenny said through tears when she was confiding in Mrs. Grant.

"I don't know why our world is so mixed up, Jenny," replied Mrs. Grant. "But Zachary already is just a normal little guy, and that's the bottom line here. We adults are the ones with this racial problem woven into our culture for years." Jenny was still crying, and the pastor's wife went on. "We all have to find solutions to the consequences of our struggles. Hopefully, we learn some things from our mistakes. I'm just so glad you chose to keep Zachary. He's going to be such a blessing for all of us; in fact, he already has brought a lot of healing into our church family. We've had to get serious about a lot of the racial issues we've been able to avoid up until now in this valley."

She reached for Jenny's hands and they prayed together. Jenny was floored when Mrs. Grant prayed for Zachary's father.

"I guess it never occurred to me to pray for him; I've just wished I'd never gone on that date with him," Jenny said as she left the day care center. She was loaded down with Chelsea, Zachary, and all their paraphernalia.

"Thanks for caring about us," she called out over her shoulder as she headed home for the day.

~~~~~~

One day when Vic stopped by Lola's Café for his mid-morning cup of coffee, his old friend, Frank Souter, slid into the booth across from him. They had known each other since boyhood, and had been in many scrapes together over the years. They always had lots of laughs when they happened to cross paths like they had this morning. They "this'd and that'd" for their first cup of coffee. When their second cup was poured, Frank stirred in his usual three spoonfuls of sugar and leaned toward Vic.

"Tell me what's going on with Jenny, Vic."

"Well, Frank, there's not much to tell. She's got two kids, very little money, and nowhere to live. Stella and I have been trying to help her until she can recover from this last baby's arrival."

"So how long do you suppose that's going to take. Vic? You think she's just going to keep having kids, and you and Stella are going to have to keep taking care of them?"

"We just figure this is the best place to put our time and money right now," said Vic as he slowly stirred his coffee.

"Well, come on, Vic. You and Stella got some dibs on your time and money now that you're getting so old." They both smiled because Vic was 5 months older than Frank.

"I'm going to level with you, Vic," snorted Frank. "I sure wouldn't want to be raising no black kid under my roof. You know what I mean, Vic. This boy is going to be a burr under your saddle from now on. You can take that to the bank. I just don't think you should be doing this to your wife and Darcy. It just ain't right."

Vic inhaled deeply on his cigarette, then slowly mashed it into the old red plastic ashtray between them before he responded to Frank. Frank knew better than to rush Vic.

"Frank, you've known me forever, and you remember how we used to go out drinking and fighting and all that. Busting lips and noses used to be our way to settle the score. Since I became a Christian a few years back, you know I've tried to put my violent side behind me. But with God as my witness, I'm telling you, Frank, right now I want to come across this table at you." He leveled an icy-cold glare at Frank.

Frank was speechless. He gulped a time or two, then tried to repair this sudden rift between him and his long-term friend.

"Look, calm down, Vic! I don't mean no harm to you and Stella. I just thought you ought to know what folks around here are talking about. That's all."

"No, that's not all, Frank. That's my grandson you're talking about. He's just as white as he is black, but what difference does a skin color make anyway, Frank? You're a shade or two darker than I am!"

Frank was speechless.

"It's our business if we want to help Jenny raise her boy. I don't need your advice about this. You can't tell me anything Stella and I haven't already struggled with since this deal about Zachary started. We know what people are saying. Stella's about worried herself sick."

"You see, Vic! Stella doesn't deserve this. Look, I'm concerned about you two. I just wanted to know how you feel about raising those bastard kids of Jenny's. I think you should put your foot down about it, man."

Vic stood up and tossed money for his coffee on the table. He leaned over close to Frank's nose and said, "Back off, Frank. I know what I'm doing. You want to know how I feel? OK, I'll tell you. I intend to keep on providing a place for my wife and family. Zachary's only problem boils down to what folks like you keep saying about him. Why don't you come around sometime and meet him. He's the cutest kid on the block."

Vic turned and started to walk away. He whirled back to Frank and added, "One more thing: before you come over, I'd appreciate an apology for what you called my grand-kids."

Frank knew Vic was serious. "You got it, Vic. You know I love Stella and you, and I sure haven't meant no harm. I'm sorry I put this one on you."

He reached for Vic's hand. "I shouldn't have said what I did about Jenny's kids." The two old friends left with a handshake, but with their friendship a bit fragile. Frank sat and stirred his cold coffee for a long time after Vic stormed out.

Later on that day, Frank was overheard talking to some workmen at his Home Designs Trailer Company. The topic of the new baby at Vic's house came up.

"Wait a minute, fellas," said Frank. "That's Dabney's grandson, and they're trying to help Jenny with a tough situation. We'd best help them raise that boy, and not be so hard on him. That baby is doing the best he can."

There were some dark looks exchanged, but finally someone said, "Well, I reckon everyone deserves a chance in this world."

So Zachary with his warm black eyes and beautiful skin became a regular part of Little River. For now, the town was settled on what the Dabneys were determined to do for this new arrival.

Send To / **Attachments**

LatimerPNG@sopac.org

Subject: Hello, you two

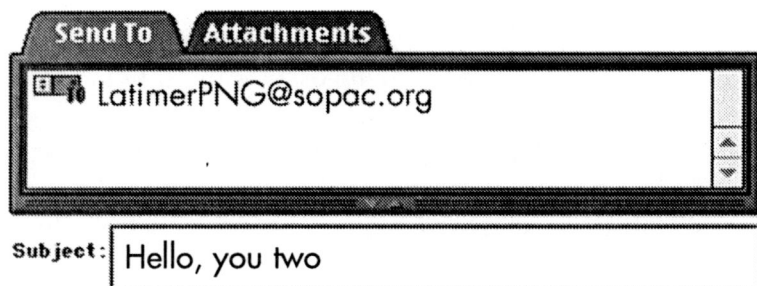

The phone call was great. It added at least 10 yrs. to Mom's life! I should've known that Dr. Chuck, Inc. would take that whole new world over there right in stride. Of course, here at the LOV parsonage, we think it is all because we pray for you every morning along with the Cheerios. I know God has a great ministry planned for you there.

When will the clinic be up and going? I'm pretty sure you are already doctoring even though the doors haven't officially opened. Sure wish I were there to help.

I ran in to Stefan Gentry the other day, and he was all questions. I gave him your e-mail address, so you will probably hear from him. It sounds like he and Ellen will announce their engagement pretty soon.....he's definitely in 'luuuuuuv.' He said they might come over to help you out next summer.

Seeing Stef reminded me of that first story I wrote a long time ago about you two in medical school. Just in case you don't remember it, I'll attach it to this e-mail—-after I edit it some more! You could say that I have added a "colorful dimension." Hold onto your hat!

By the way, I know neither of us can do daily e-mails like some folks do. Some days I don't even check mine. Just let us hear from you off and on, and that will be good enough for us. We'll try to do the same. Now that we have your mission station phone number, the pressure is off of everyone. Due to the cost, I don't think you'll be hearing from us via telephone unless it is a genuine emergency.

So, e-mail is the thing. I promise not to send you a bunch of junk mail. Be thankful because I really get a load of that stuff from all over the place. Why do people think I need this constant influx of cerebral pollution? Maybe 1 in 50 is worth saving for a sermon or maybe an ice-breaker.

Be sure and let us know if some of your info to us should be on the QT. You know I'm good at confidentiality, now that I've been in the ministry awhile. But I'm also good at spreading the news about how you all are doing over there. You won't believe how many people ask me how things are going for Dr. Chuck.

Bye for now! Sounds like Trudy needs some help with her honey–do list. I'm excited......

Jesus' love,
Wayne

```
┌─────────────────────────────────────────────┐
│ ▛Send To▜▛Attachments▜                        │
│ ┌─────────────────────────────────────────┐ ▲│
│ ▐ Definitely Limited                       │ ▲│
│ └─────────────────────────────────────────┘ ▼│
└─────────────────────────────────────────────┘
```

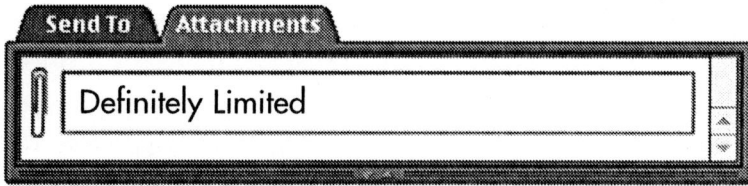

DEFINITELY LIMITED

I.

The two medical students pushed their plastic trays down the cafeteria line. These two, Stefan Gentry and Chuck Latimer, had been friends since middle school in Little River. They were not only bonded by all their boyhood adventures, but also by their families' friendship. Both families faithfully attended the Lily of the Valley Community Church. As boys, they had passed notes during endless sermons and had mutually disrupted countless other church functions. Together they had always dreamed of being doctors, and now they found themselves in the midst of their dream and staring at each other in weariness.

This was their first break since midnight. They reached for black coffee and stale doughnuts, and were hoping to stay awake until their shift was over. When that was done, and before they could leave and get some sleep, they still had a consult to sit in on with two of their professors. Their assignment in the mental wards was coming to a close. They were bone-weary, ready for a change in their training, but fascinated in a dull, early morning way by the psychiatric wards.

After sitting in silence a few minutes, Chuck ventured a question. "Stef, remember those church stories we used to hear about God and demons and all that?"

"You know," Stefan replied, "I'm not sure what I believe about all that now. We learned about all that at Lily of the

Valley, but right now that seems a long way off."

"Yeah, I guess you mentioned that awhile back. Just forget it," replied Chuck. He stirred his coffee, and dreaded the first sip of the warmed over brew often served up before the breakfast cooks punched in.

"So, why are you asking?" Stefan replied after a few more moments of silence between them.

"Oh, I just think about that stuff sometimes, Stef. Look, let's just leave it alone." Chuck was surprised at how gruff and impatient he sounded.

"Nope. Come on now, why are you asking me about demons? There must be a reason?"

Chuck took a deep breath. "Well, OK. Do you really think that there might be demons functioning today?" He raised his hand to Stefan who was about to reply. "Now, I'm talking beyond the ghost story mentality here, man."

"You're kidding! Today, in medical school, you're asking me this? Do I need this, Chuck?" Stefan was also in a less than gracious mood.

"Yeah, well, it freaks people out to even mention it around here. But I thought you might have some choice comments for me. We did hear a lot about this, as I recall?"

"You mean tiny little bad guys with forks and tails?" Stefan was resorting to sarcasm.

"No, Stef, you scuz! Not Halloween stuff. Look, I mean the real thing....like major bad, evil beings. It seems like some of those poor folks up in the unit are controlled by something much bigger than they are. It's wicked. Some patients would truly like to change, get out of here, and have a life. But they can't. We've observed this in our training, Stef. It's like they catch the ball but can't run with it. I mean, even when they really try to rein it all in, they can't make it work."

"I know, Chuck. It's weird, isn't it? But I'm not sure about the demonic being a part of all that."

"Well, some patients have gone home and come back to re-nurse their emotions in just this six weeks we've been around. And they don't get much better when they go through their second round of treatment."

"But, that's just life for some folks, Dr. Latimer. It's about bad environment, peer pressure, rotten parents, drugs, chemical imbalance, and the whole ball of wax that makes people wacko inside their skulls. Didn't you soak up anything on the shrinks' grand rounds, bud?"

"I know, I know! I'm not arguing about what we've learned, Stef. I mean beyond all that." Chuck pushed his stale coffee away with a look of disgust. "Give me a break."

There was a low whistle over the other coffee cup. "You are...yeah, you really are seriously wondering about all this, aren't you. And I know you aren't dumb. So, just let this soak in. You think this satanic thing is viable. You think patients here may be under some sort of outer space control or something?"

"I'm just saying, I wonder about this stuff sometimes."

II

The lavender metallic smudge pots bubbled smugly along the high shelves that covered the stone walls of the vast hall. The smell and the smoke from the pots permeated everything in the room, but no one seemed concerned about the choking atmosphere. Mammoth tapestries, now tattered, once beautiful, hung over the molding walls. Faded rugs of the same quality covered the warm, clammy floors. An atmosphere of tension was felt as soon as one entered the room. Something was not quite right. And all energies must strive. . . .strive. . . .strive to sustain that magnificent error.

At the end of the cavernous room, a conference area was set up with chairs and a long table. It was a place designed for people of importance. At the head of the table was an enormous wing chair that dominated its surroundings. It was silver with lavender velvet upholstery. As a matter of fact, the whole room at one time must have been carefully decorated in a wealth of lavenders and silvers. It was indeed elegant.....once upon a time.

At the other end of the long room was an elaborate but functional desk piled high with papers, folders, maps, weather charts, and all other manner of confusion. This clutter kept sliding and spilling over onto the floor. A scrawny secretary of sorts hovered over the desk as he constantly straightened the array of papers and documents. He had worked himself into a near frenzy with little success. The littering and straightening process continued endlessly.

Others were in the room, all under pressure, all feverishly at work. Their clothing gave the impression of rich court life. Their brocades, laces, buckles, and satins glimmered in the dim light of the smudge pots. At the same time, the smoke from the pots made it rather difficult to see anything at all. Upon closer examination, the clothing was tattered, much like costumes from a second rate theater production. The first impression of elegance was given, but in reality, the costumes were only cheap, worn out imitations.

Those who wore the clothing were constantly adjusting seams, tucking in loose ends, pulling at threads, and trying to show off only the best side of their attire. It was their job, when not concerned with appearances, to polish and refill the smudge pots along the shelves; this they accomplished with the help of long poles and ladders. Each one hoped that soon he would be noticed for his diligence and moved to a more distinguished area of service.

Sidelong glances were constantly directed toward a huge door just beyond the ornate lavender chair. It was not unusual for one to fall from his ladder perch while preening and peeking at the door. This always caused a horrible con-

fusion of lavender smoke, clanging metal, and angry accusations about the fallen one's lack of ability to do this or any other job. It was rather amusing to hear the distressed workers trying to curse in a dignified manner. They knew they had to watch their language.

The secretary was now feverishly shuffling documents over his desk. It was apparent that his efforts had not brought to light what he wanted, whatever that was. Confusion still reigned. Time was running out. Finally, he broke silence and complained loudly that his plans for the day, which he had so carefully drawn up yesterday in order to be fully prepared today, were now lost. And he couldn't even find the outlines given to him by his superior about tactics for today.

"Things won't be going well, especially at that hospital," he sputtered. "Well, no one's perfect. I'll just have to do a bit of improvisation here." His nervous humming was no cover for his rapidly diminishing confidence.

As a matter of fact, things were frequently lost, and without explanation. When occasionally a stack of his lost documents was found, it was usually too late for him to do anything to rescue the situation. The secretary was rather sure that one of the smudge tenders on the ladders was secretly sabotaging his job.

"Some people will do anything to get ahead," he fumed. He must someday find time to humiliate this employee in front of the others. How sweet to plan revenge!

This momentary distraction brought a smirk to his face, but this he quickly concealed from the others in the room. He dare not appear unprofessional. At last a brief outline of what was to be done was re-drawn, and some archaic maps were unearthed from the tattered files. Some hasty orders were shouted out. And none too soon.

With a screeching clang, the huge metal door at the end of the room was wrenched open. The one who paused in the doorway was awesome: L. Arch Fiend. He was obviously the one for whom the room and its contents existed. The secretary, with his crumpled outline giving him what he hoped was an air of preparedness, swept himself into a courtly bow over his tarnished buckles. The others scrambled down from their ladders, and with scathing looks at one another, assumed similar poses of obeisance. They knew the secretary had somehow come up through the ranks to amount to something, so they slavishly copied his airs.

"Sire!" was the greeting from all their lips.

A brief pause at the door was the only greeting from L. Arch Fiend to those who worked in the room. With an air of pomp and dignity, he swept his purple velvet robes around the closing door, and strode to the huge silver chair to begin his day. Behind him, the echo of the clanging door resounded into what must've been an endless opening.

The sound slowly died away.

The frantic atmosphere of the room clung to L. Arch Fiend like a shriveled skin. He was constant work, continual frustration, and utmost dedication to a task. It was as if he were their source.

He was elegant beyond imagination; timeworn, perhaps, but without doubt a handsome and commanding figure. The purple of his robes suited his regal demeanor. Added to this, he wore a look of hardness that comes only through long and wearing experience. The attempt to cover the tarnished grandeur he shared with his surroundings had been rather well accomplished. Of this, he was immensely proud.

With a bored glance at the smudge pots, he inquired, "Bickerz, have all the smudges been on time and working this morning?"

"Yes, sire!" snapped the secretary. "The smoke screen is well in place. Also, a multitude of other significant things are concealed and camouflaged. I am very pleased to report that the hospital that you were concerned about is definitely *secured. And everything is under surveillance as you ordered last evening."*

He nodded his approval. Never had anyone heard him use the word, 'good,' nor were they allowed to use such words themselves.

"And do you have that Daily Detail Report ready for me?"

"Not quite ready, Sire," he continued brightly. "I do have the basics. I have them right here," he ended his sentence with a flourish of the hand which held the crumpled outlines.

"The Daily Detail Report, Bickerz?" the supreme commander snarled.

"Sir, I'm just now firming up the outline. That detailed report that I wrote out last evening must be under this stack somewhere..."

"Bickerz! Do not give me any of your sniveling, stupid excuses this morning." In a lowered voice, he added, "And don't call me 'sir.' You know 'sire' sounds much better in front of the other employees. We've talked about this before."

Bickerz gulped and tried in vain to swallow his humiliation. He knew the smudges were enjoying this scene at his expense. L. Arch Fiend paced up and down the clammy marble until he regained his composure.

"Well!" he harrumphed, "Since you seem to have lost everything of importance from yesterday, what is on YOUR agenda for this morning, Bickerz?" was the syrupy question.

"Sire," announced Bickerz "Those of us who work constantly in here, all of us, thought some redecorating and refurbishing might be in order." This was said with a look of feigned appreciation toward the smudges. They knew, of course, that he was actually hoping to distract his superior from his blunders of the morning.

"Re...what? Refurbish? Whatever for?"

"Well, it does become rather depressing when things are

never renewed. And even one's clothing must be replaced once in awhile, mustn't it?"

Through clenched teeth came the reply, "It is no wonder you lose the significant while muddling around with your pet projects, Bickerz. We owe every precious minute to the conspiracy, and here you are dawdling around with such pettiness. Utter inanity. As if I didn't have enough to concern me right now!" He paused and surveyed the room.

"Well, I suspect we have conceived a corporate plan? And you, Bickerz, with your usual alacrity, are ready to present it, I assume? So, proceed."

Bickerz thought this change of direction tantamount to a display of affection. He was fluffing up his own interior a bit in response. Maybe his superior was beginning to recognize his good..no? Wrong word! "True?" Oops, still not the word! Try.... "distinctive" taste. With a flattered smile, Bickerz bustled over to a corner file cabinet from which he smoothly pulled out a very thick, well organized folder full of fabric samples and paint charts. The insignificant was always so easy to locate.

"If you please, sire? Here is our basic plan. We thought we could clear out all this old furniture, and transform this room into a contemporary showpiece. You know, with stainless steel, glass, smooth wood panels, and with some classy, contemporary art pieces. Originals, of course."

A look of sheer disgust came over the face of L. Arch Fiend. "What are you proposing? You want to change all this obvious elegance for a passing fad of bleak design and slavish innovation? I think not!" was the haughty response.

"But, sire, some of the ideas your staff has proposed will improve our procedures as well as our surroundings," ventured Bickerz cautiously. "The smudges would like to update their processes by using some of the more modern military diversionary procedures. We could get rid of these archaic smudge pots, and maybe even update our computers?"

"I cannot imagine what insanity has brought you to this point, Bickerz. And that goes for all of you," he was glaring at the smudges. "I thought by now you were all aware and thoroughly trained in what we are all about?"

"But, Excellency, this would help us accomplish the purpose that we all hold so dear. The issue here is that we must not lag behind in modern technology."

Bickerz whined with authority as he adopted what he hoped was a very cosmopolitan and sophisticated expression, "Forgive me, sire, but we must find some new avenues of approaching our truth...uh...I mean, our goals."

"Bickerz, you twit! You expect ME to forgive? You are a lunatic!" he shrieked. He was again pacing up and down the length of the huge room. "I cannot conceive of what you have just said, but since you used the word,...it is precisely the truth that we are striving to avoid. Get rid of! Twist, twist, TWIST!"

His voice rose in a piercing crescendo. "Now listen to me. Maintain this place like it is and always has been, baroque through and through. The fancier the better. It looks more valuable that way. Besides if they are old, things seem to have intrinsic value."

With an oily smirk he said hoarsely, "Oh, I love that concept, 'things with intrinsic value.'" The words slid off his tongue as he laughed. "Now scrap all this wasted time of yours, all of you, and let's get down to some bonafide, smarmy business for today."

Bickerz sighed, then agreed, "Yes, sire." He knew there was probably more pontificating to come from his superior.

"One more thing, Bickerz," said L. Arch Fiend. "Just remember, while we are on the subject of appearances, let outside trappings go unless they will capture a mind! Concentrate on the mind! The Mind...now there's the real battleground." His leather-gloved fist landed with a loud crash on the conference table. Everyone in the hall flinched.

"There is, however, another angle, Bickerz. Sometimes if people are involved with exterior issues, their minds become an easier prey (Careful! That's with an "e" not an "a"). For instance, I have always considered a day spent trapped in a behind-schedule beauty shop an excellent diversionary tactic with females. Watch the fury kick in at awesome levels! My! My! Temper, Temper! Tsk, Tsk! I just love it! Remember that one, my dear Bickerz."

"Yes, sire," said Bickerz to the departing commander. He realized that he would have to return to his job of patching up these old, tattered things. His role was just so much hovering over cracks in the veneer. It was to be more of the same old story, but then, there was gratification involved in his life's calling if one looked closely. He did have leadership responsibilities and no one but L. Arch Fiend told him what to do.

And! He had just been called, "my dear Bickerz!" Well, at least he had been clever enough to momentarily distract the leadership from the loss of the daily plans. Brilliant! His humming brightened up a bit.

"You, up there!" he shouted at the smudge perched on the tallest ladder. Now that he had his concentration back he realized that the smoke screen was losing its density. "Two of your pots are out of smoke!" The ladder teetered precariously, and Bickerz began to scribble down what he could remember from the plans he had written down yesterday.

"Let's see. Legion #335 must be near that boy's room by now. They'll make their moves quickly now," he muttered. Louder, he stated with as much authority as he could muster after being so flattered and distracted, "Don't let me down now, my smudgies."

III.

In the mental wards of Riverton General Hospital, Donny Transome awakened with a start. Opening his eyes enough to see the dawn coming, he fell back onto his pillow. There seemed to be a purple haze filtering through the room with the coming daylight. To his chagrin, his mind was churning within seconds. There'd be no more sleep today.

Donny Transome had already completed more therapy than most people undergo in a lifetime. His struggles with life had begun at an early age and had continued into his high school career. His parents and teachers were at a loss. For too long they had tried everything they knew to try help Donny.

Donny mulled over his stay at this hospital. For him, the place had become necessary for living. He had been brought here after an unsuccessful try at suicide. Well, it was successful, but one of his buddies found him before the massive dose of drugs could take his life. For several months, he had tried to adjust his mental confusion and emotional wasteland to some sort of functional pattern.

At one time, the pattern seemed established and he felt secure enough to return to his world outside the hospital. But, slowly, the confusion returned, and the purple haze of dreams and conflicts reclaimed him. His parents feared another time of self-destruction, and brought him back to this place of safety. Here, the staff would not let him hurt himself, and for that, he was profoundly thankful even though it was hard for him to admit he needed their help. He knew he had to command the hurt on the inside, but surrendering to the healing process was still terrifying. Often, he still felt caught by the dilemma that raged inside him.

Today, he was to come to some conclusions concerning his future. Either he moved to another institution for an indefinite period of time, "Like the rest of my life," he thought wryly. Or he could once again try to live on the outside. They had done all they could for him in this treatment center.

The past kept making inroads with which the present could not cope. The agony still growled around inside him. It was indeed a frightening time for him. It called up within him all sorts of conflicts. Today it was particularly difficult to think straight about his future. If he could just quit thinking about his past failures and problems; but, for some reason, he could not keep his emotional wheels from churning in reverse. And they were stirring up a purple dust.

IV.

Bickerz felt confident. He had not thought things would go this well. After all, he was culpable for the loss of all their previous plans for this hospital, and these spur of the moment procedures always have some hidden weak spots. He was glad that Legion #335 had remembered to use the specter of the past for the frontal attack on Donny. And of course, the smudges had gone above and beyond the call of duty to keep the screen up. They realized it was their necks along with his that were at stake.

What a picture of teamwork, and now one almost permanently under their control. Fabulous. Should be just a matter of time until that consultation with Donny and his team of doctors was a closed chapter. One big victory at the hospital and L. Arch Fiend would be much easier to live with.

Momentarily distracted from his overseeing, Bickerz mused. He wondered what the "L." stood for? Once had he bravely ventured a question in that direction, and in a rare moment of confidence, his superior told him, "Only One ever used that name. I do not like it or its memories. No more questions. I think as little as possible about crashing into this place I now inhabit. It is best to forget one's past, after all, isn't it?"

V.

Donny realized with a start that he was going to be late. He would so like to skip this meeting with his doctor and therapist, and all those med students. Suddenly he felt overwhelmed and like it was useless to try any more. But, he knew he would have to face them sooner or later.

~~

"Keep that screen thick and heavy up in the boy's wing. It's looking good from here," chirped Bickerz as he consulted his archaic computer screen and grabbed some maps before they slipped onto the floor. He hoped no one had noticed his daydreaming about his relationship with L. Arch Fiend. After all, it was just a brief distraction from the business at hand. He couldn't help it if it seemed like he and His Excellence were becoming friends. It just felt so warm and special, and thinking about it always broke his concentration as he relished his thoughts.

~~

As Donny hurried to dress, he continued the mental rehearsal of his past. His treatment team had been telling him that functioning was possible for him; but, at the same time, they gently encouraged him that only he could put his life together. They would continue to monitor his medications, and to provide support and therapy, but he could no longer continue his dependence upon them on a daily basis. Well, if they felt that he was ready to move forward, maybe their trust in him was worth checking into.

"At least I hope it is," Donny whispered as he walked heavily out of his room. "I sure do hope so." Sunshine suddenly flooded the hallways as he walked along by the big picture windows. He noticed that new flowers had been planted around the atrium in the center of the building. He also was aware that the purple dawn was receding.

~~

"Hope!?" screamed Bickerz. "Look out there, you idiot. You, up on the frontal ladder, re-light your pots at once. That screen at the hospital is dying out!"

Everyone cringed at Bickerz's screams and shouts. More pots were hurriedly brought in. The smudges obviously were trying. The frontal ladder began to sway and bend with the added load. Then, in a heartbeat, it happened. There was a horrendous crash as a whole shelf of smudge pots crashed to the floor. Purple smoke hissed along the molding walls and along the cracks in the floor....useless.

It would take hours to clean up the mess and get the smoke screen up again. Some of the old smudge pots were destroyed. And the smudges were all cursing and blaming one another at the same time. It was truly an inferno of tempers. The cleanup was not helped by their determination to find a scapegoat for their collective mishap.

Bickerz, equally determined to avoid the blame, shouted, "Now you've really done it. The smoke screen is seriously compromised. Get this mess out of the way. Send the broken pots out for repairs. No doubt, we'll all catch it over this one. And we'll be late for the noon meal. By the time we arrive, there won't be a scrap worth eating. You'll be lucky to get anything at all after this blunder."

Actually, he was quite pleased. This disaster, horrible as it was, meant that L. Arch Fiend would no longer be after his hide about the lost plans for the day. There were some gratifying elements in this rotten day after all. He mumbled distractedly about his luncheon plans as he put on a front of helping with the smoldering mess. This sort of work really was beneath him, but he liked to act helpful in order to keep team spirits up at a time like this. His atonal humming never stopped.

VI.

The small conference room at the end of the hall looked as if it had been used for several meetings without cleaning. Out of date magazines lay scattered on the lumpy couches against the wall. Chairs were ill-arranged around a scratched table. There was a litter of candy wrappers and half-filled drink cups on the table. Empty bottled water containers were everywhere. It was not a pretty room, but it was well used, and critical things happened here.

The room was hurriedly straightened. Soon two doctors arrived, a man and a woman. They had spent countless hours with Donny Transome, who was now several minutes late for their conference. Their expressions showed their concern; their conversations reflected their professional attitudes and expertise. The woman reached for the house phone on the table.

"Send in Gentry and Latimer as soon as they check back in on the ward, please. I think they're just coming off their break. And see if you can find Donny Transome. He's late for our meeting." Her voice was pleasant though raspy. She was used to making requests and expecting them to be carried out.

As Donny approached the conference room, he paused outside the door. Blinking several times, he realized that the purplish haze of conflicts which had dogged him for days was barely there. At least maybe he could think straight for a change. That thought in itself gave him the courage to open the door and walk in.

~~

The smudges worked feverishly with their own brand of courage to get the smoke screen going again, a difficult thing to do when they had already put in a lot of hard work that morning. If "The Bick," their term of affection used for their supervisor behind his back, had not messed up the pre-

sentation for the new renovations, they might have had a chance at a major upgrade. Certainly, they needed to replace this archaic pot bubbling system with some modern procedures. And if the consult at the hospital had started on time, everything would have been over with before this antiquated shelf had collapsed. Now, no fault of theirs, nothing was working out....no, not even lunch.

Probably Bickerz would punish them by cutting off their food completely. This was his favorite punishment when things did not function up to the standards of the front office. Someday, they would gang up on him, and then he would know what it was like to be shouted at and never appreciated.

~~

Just before Donny's arrival, the other doctor lowered his head and momentarily closed his eyes. His colleague glanced quickly at him; it concerned her that his weariness would show up at a time like this when they needed to be sharp. Donny's future was a stake, but it was also an important time of observation and training for the students who would be joining them. She cleared her throat and shuffled her papers with the hope of getting her partner's head back in the room with her and up to speed with their process.

~~

"Oh, piss!!!! He's praying!!!!" was all that was distinguishable from the plethora of oaths that burbled forth from Bickerz. The remaining pots began to hiss instead of bubble, and the lilac haze was diminishing rapidly. His shrieks brought everyone in the room back to the feverish pitch of working frantically for their cause. Bickerz even began trying to re-light some of the pots himself. But either his matches were too damp or his hands too sweaty and shaky to help very much. He had known for some time that he needed one of those modern little butane lighters for emergencies like this one.

"But, noooo...keep everything the same. Keep using matches! 'Don't change anything,' " he mimicked his superior and all but snarled.

VII.

The meeting went overtime, but when it was over, the room emptied quickly. The doctors ushered Donny to the door, and wished him well as he re-entered his life. As Donny left, they smiled at each other as only those can who have shared and won a great battle against huge odds. The medical students, trying to act like part of the professional scene, busily scribbled a few notes before leaving. They all four shook hands as they left the room.

So, Donny was released...dismissed...free...and surprised by the outcome of the consultation. He was not sure until he began to talk with his team of professionals today that he was ready for this. The more they all had talked, the more he knew he wanted to leave and move on with his life. It didn't look at all easy to take the big step to leave; but, to make his life work, he knew he must try out the life skills he had been working on with his therapists.

He was glad that the medical team would continue to monitor his progress, and that they had found a support group of boys his age for him to join. He had never prayed much, but he found himself thanking God that the session had gone so well. It felt miraculous.

Donny went back to his room after calling home from the pay phone in the day room. Even after all he had put them through, his parents seemed pleased that he could come home. His mother said they would come for him as soon as they could shut down the service station and change into clean clothes.

Somehow, Donny felt more hopeful about this homecoming. He had been able to shed the staggering dread that he had felt during previous sessions with his treatment team. With a smile, he decided he'd call his girlfriend, Jenny. She might like to see what a real, live, mental patient looked like later on tonight. So he'd better pack his things and say his good-byes.

~~

Bickerz, bedraggled from his day of janitorial work and failure at the hospital, was busily scribbling out a set of new orders for Legion #335, the diligent loyalists who had remained on duty over at the mental wards. It looked like a new patient had arrived and was presenting with some wonderful possibilities for messing up in a major way.

"Just the way we like to see them come in," he hummed under his breath. "There's never a dull moment around here." He still had not eaten, but he dutifully continued to work alone in the deserted room. Lunch suddenly seemed immaterial with the stakes up so high again at the hospital admittance office. And he knew that a big flourish at the beginning of this new case would make an enormous impression on L. Arch Fiend.

~~

As Chuck and Stefan walked out into the daylight together, they mulled over the consult they had just witnessed.

"That man is so capable," said Chuck. "He really pulled it all together for that guy, didn't he?"

"I thought Transome did it? Did I miss something?" asked Stefan.

"Yeah, well, you know what I mean. When the kid was ready, the old doc was in there with the clincher. Sort of like connecting the dots so that the picture comes out right," Chuck observed. They both shivered up against the brisk wind blowing out of the cloudless sky.

Chuck continued, "It looks like there is some hope for

Donny now. If he can just forget the past and get.....”

"Nope," interrupted Stefan, "remember what the lady-doc said about forgetting and forgiveness?"

"Why don't you refresh me? I know you are going to anyway," replied a less than happy Chuck.

"Well, OK! She said forgiveness has to come before anyone can move on from all that bad stuff in the right way. Otherwise, it is just repression and denial," Stefan added in a blasé tone of voice. Then he added a disclaimer, "At least, that's what I heard her say."

"Cripes, Stef! Could you back off?" Chuck was not just a little ticked off. He changed his tune as they continued walking. "Well, it sure will take a lot of whatever it takes to get over all Donny has been through. Man, what a beginning in life."

The two slouched along in silence. Stefan spoke first. "You still thinking about big, bad, red gremlins?"

"Look, I was just trying to mix it up a little...just giving you a hard time. I know you don't like to get into stuff like that," Chuck said as he tried to cover for embarrassing himself earlier with his inane theological comments and questions.

"But, now you've started me thinking about it all! Me! The campus scientific guru," groused Stefan. "Maybe I'm losing my grip due to lack of sleep."

"No lie? Well, well! Let me know what you come up with. See you next round. By the way, you're seriously grouchy, Stef. Get some rest, man!"

"Same to you, fella," Stef muttered under his breath,

Chuck waved and yawned as his bus drew up to the curb. He stepped over the snowmelt and onto his bus. The gutter was running with an iridescent, purplish slush.

~~

Donny's doctor walked back into the conference room after the others left. He sat down for a moment on one of the lumpy couches, and rested his head in his hands. The others had no idea how often he prayed. It was what he did when the buck stopped on him, and he needed a solution. Sometimes he was at the end of his skills and knowledge, and there was no other place to turn. At those times, prayer seemed very logical to him. Even scientific..

Things had gone well today, and he was proud of Donny Transome. He loved it when a troubled kid was able to pick up the pieces of his or her puzzle, and make a stab at moving on with life. As the doctor sat there, he took a moment to pray that the pieces of that puzzle stayed in place for Donny. Frankly, he had some doubts, especially since everything came together so quickly today. But, he knew that the boy had every right to keep trying and keep learning. If he messed up, he'd be back, but perhaps in the process, he would learn something from his attempts at having a life.

The other doctor needed him down the hall in admitting. A new patient was being checked in, and she had asked him to help with the intake review. The girl was presenting as a known addict, and she had been caught having sex with another girl in the locker room after school. Both doctors knew they had their work cut out for them. Slowly, he pushed himself up from the couch and ran his hands through his hair.

"On to the next page," he cajoled himself. "God, am I having fun yet?"

As he closed the door to the conference room behind him, he smiled and said out loud, "You know what, God? I really am!" He looked around sheepishly to see if anyone had overheard him. He did not want anyone in the mental unit at Riverton General Hospital to see him smiling and talking into thin air to some sort of deity.

VIII.

The iron door clanged shut with a whoosh of hot air and cinders behind L. Arch Fiend. With it's echo were heard his moans of frustration.

"Damn the limitations! Why!? Why!? All this humiliation and loss over a doctor's shitty little prayer? Over a hoodlum's word like 'hope?' Damn Bickerz and his precocious little team of sniggering buddies! Damn everything!!" His deep purple frothing became a smoldering part of the diminishing echo.

Bickerz smoothed his bruised ego, tried to appear organized, and looked the other way.

Send To **Attachments**

LatimerPNG@sopac.org

Subject: Heavy Questions

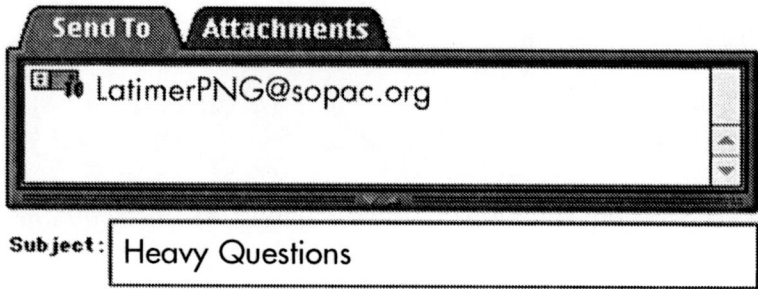

Thanks for reading the "ltd!" story. I predicted you'd come to full attention and call the SWAT team to come after me when you read all the "woo-woo" stuff that I added to the story about the mental wards.

But, don't you ever wonder what's going on in the heavenlies when we struggle here on earth? Wouldn't you just love to peek under that curtain in the stars once in awhile? Maybe God and Satan were having a discussion re. Donny Transome when he was about to meet with his team that day. You know, like Job's story?

Surely you know that I was "just playing" with the idea of L. Arch Fiend's "war room?" That is total imagination! I hardly think anyone is going to start a whole new genre of demonology about Satan's domain based on this story. It's a story, OK?

You can make fun of my story, or come up with a better one in your spare time. That's a challenge, and I know how you like to win. Go for it.

We put some trinkets etc. in snail mail today for your kids to share with their new friends. It's just a box of stuff from the Dollar Store. One of the Sunday School classes wanted a missions' project, so this seemed like a good idea. Hope you agree...it cost more to mail the package than all the trinkets put together.

Sam Loftis chipped in for the postage. What a great guy. Looks like their son, Joel, may be coming back to

Little River to coach over at the high school. He was great with the big city schools, but missed the small town atmosphere. Now if he can figure out how to have a family, he may be willing to settle down. I know Nora is ready for some grandchildren. I hear their cottage out at the lake has been turned into a really nice retirement place for them.

Trudy just said "Hi, over there!" Time for bed...Bye for now.

Hugs all around,
Wayne

P. S. Since I've finished another LOV story, I'll attach it to this e-mail. This one was definitely a pleasure to write, and you'll remember all the characters. I think Laurie will really like this one...let her read it first.

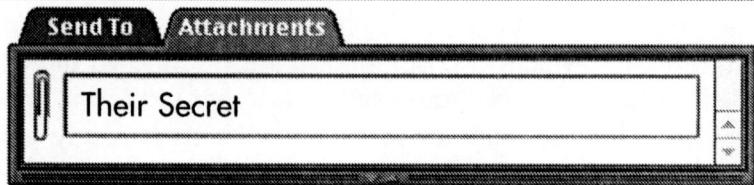

Send To | **Attachments**

| Their Secret

THEIR SECRET

They were wonder-struck, for lack of a better term. Who'd have dreamt that they could be open about their love for one another? For years, their connection had been strong, but now they could smile openly at one another, hold hands as long as they wanted, even watch sunrises and sunsets together.

Of course, they were used to their agreement, but this freedom gave their secret a new dimension. They communicated on their own frequency, and it was all built on years of trust and commitment to marriage. Now this carefully protected relationship could be colored with hues of reality instead of the black and white patterns of the past.

It all began when Max and Lida were in high school. They'd been in school and church together all their lives, but their romance began in high school. He was the mid-teen athletic wonder, and she was the blossoming, dewy beauty; he, the quarterback and she, the cheerleader. He wore her ring on his pinkie finger, and she wore his gold football on a chain.

When graduation came, Max and Lida knew that any marriage plans would have to be set aside awhile for college. They didn't want marriage to hinder Max's dream of becoming a surgeon. Max received the football scholarship of his dreams at his father's alma mater on the other side of the USA, and Lida went to college within driving distance of Little River. Athletes were blessed with scholarships to big universities, and beauties were expected to pay their own way.

Their separation was difficult, and as the year progressed, their letters and rare visits tapered off. Football consumed Max's life, and Lida caught the eye of Carter Sullivan, one of the local campus leaders. He swept her into his world of fun and activities with his confidence and promises to show her around and help her to make new friends. They both had "steadies" at home; nevertheless, pretty soon all of their spare time was spent together.

The connection between Max and Lida was abruptly severed by a pregnancy. Lida's. One frosty, winter weekend on a fraternity outing at the lake lodge, the friendship between Lida and Carter changed modes. It went from friendly to romantic to passionate. For a few weeks, the confused pair struggled to reframe their changed relationship. All they had was a brief friendship to build on.

Eventually, Lida had to confide in Carter that she was pregnant. He never faltered. He declared his commitment to her and their baby, proposed to her, and promised to make this all work out. On Spring Break when Max was involved with spring training, the unlikely pair became man and wife before a local judge and phoned their parents.

The surprise nuptials were thoroughly dissected by the members of the Lily of the Valley Community Church. The news reached Max when his father called late one night to try to let his son down gently about Lida's marriage. He made sure he had the final part of the story straight before he said, "Son, they say Lida's pregnant." Max hurt for weeks; his dream of a future with Lida was permanently gone. The thing that puzzled him the most was why Lida never let on about being serious about Carter Sullivan. A lot of his questions would have to go unanswered now.

Lida and Carter struggled to put each other through school. They both became teachers, and had four children. Their marriage was forged by hard work and prayer, by commitment to their home, by devotion to their children, and by sheer determination. Whenever things got shaky, Carter would say, "Look, I promised you we'd make this work, so let's see what we can figure out. You know we can do it, sweetheart." And Lida would join him again, and again, and again.

Rarely, did Lida let her thoughts drift back to Max. She was too busy with her babies and her teaching schedule to dwell on painful memories. Once in awhile, she heard something about him through the Lily of the Valley Church grapevine where she and Carter were teaching in the junior high department. All in all, she considered herself very fortunate to be married to a man as dependable and wise as Carter.

About Max? His football career won him All-American status, and a lot of athletic acclaim, even professional offers. But, he followed his larger game plan and went on to medical school after college. Now he was even farther away from his hometown. It took long years of training for him to become a surgeon, and during that time both of his parents died. Gradually, his home- town became more of a memory than a reality. He was totally enthralled with his medical career.

When Max was established in a surgical practice at his alma mater with a good income, he met and married a lovely, local teacher named Sally. They hurried to start their family. Their only pregnancy was twins, a boy, Stefan, and a girl, Megan. They worked diligently to provide a good home. They joined a church remarkably like the Lily of the Valley Community Church of Max's memories.

Max remembered Lida with a wince occasionally, but he didn't allow himself to dredge up all those hurt feelings. He was content with his family, and had moved on years ago from the devastating loss of his first and only other love. The flames of his high school romance were cold ashes.

Twenty years drifted by. Lida often drove over an hour to

visit her widowed mother who had moved to her small family farm in the country. Several miles on beyond the farm was an enormous new shopping mall, and sometimes Lida added a shopping spree to her routine visit.

This trip, Lida decided to run over to the mall and do some early Christmas shopping for their teenagers at the trendy stores she had heard her friends talking about. In the late afternoon, she slowed down her shopping, and stopped at a mall coffee shop with tables surrounded by twinkle-lit ficus trees. As she was checking her gift list and resting her tired feet, she felt a hand on her shoulder, and then was looking into Max's always clear blue eyes.

"Max?' was all she could manage to say. Her list fluttered to the floor.

"Hi, Lida," Max said quietly as he retrieved her shopping list. "I saw you sitting here, and I just had to say, 'Hello.' "

"What in the world are you doing out here in the middle of nowhere?" she queried. She hoped she didn't look too dumbfounded.

"I could ask you the same thing!" he smiled and went on. "I'm considering coming back home as chief surgeon at Riverton General Hospital. I'm meeting with the hospital administrators for the next few days.

"Well, that's wonderful, Max. Sounds like your dream job."

"We'll see. Right now I have a bad case of the yawns, so here I am walking around and trying to wake up. I rented a car at the airport, and just got too sleepy on the long drive over to Little River. An emergency kept me up all last night."

"Would you like to trade in your walk for some good old-fashioned caffeine?" she kidded him.

"Sure thing," he agreed, and ordered a cup of black coffee and a refill for her. They spent a long time chatting and catching up on the details of one another's lives. Finally, Max said, as he leaned back in the little bistro chair, "You know, Li, it took me the rest of college and all of medical school to finally decide it was all right to marry someone else."

Lida avoided looking up. They were silent as they both felt the pain of twenty years ago roll back over them. "What really happened to us?" He blurted out, and then quickly retreated with, "I'm sorry! I guess it's not fair to anyone to ask those questions now?"

Lida could sense rather than see his jaw flexing like it used to when he'd run onto the football field. She grinned and didn't look up. "Max, do you still do that funny thing with your jaw? Like maybe when you walk into the O.R. ready to operate? Like right now?" They both laughed. He rubbed his tight jaw, had to admit she was right, and the tension passed.

"I don't mind your question at all, Max," Lida replied. Her hazel eyes were now looking steadily into his blue ones. "What happened is part of our history, yours and mine, and always will be. We were supposed to wait for each other, and I happened to get pregnant. End of promises! Carter wanted to marry me and make us into a family. It has been a good solution. He's a fine man, Max, and a real Christian. You'll like him."

Max smiled and winked, his jaw now relaxed.

"Good, Lida. That's an answer I can accept. I'll look forward to meeting Carter someday, and I want you to meet Sally." Without a pause he finished his coffee and said, "You'd better get back to being Mrs. Santa Claus. And I need to be on my way, or I'll lose my room reservation and be late for my first interview."

"I need to leave, too. I've done enough damage for one trip to the mall." She began to gather up her shopping bags. The mall carillon had already chimed 5 o'clock.

"Here. Let me carry those out to your car for you," offered Max. They bundled up against a gentle snow, and walked out to the end of the parking lot where she'd left her car earlier in the afternoon. Max helped her load up her car, then reached in with her keys to start her car warming up for the drive home.

"It's been so good to see you, Max. Maybe you and Sally can come back to the Lily of the Valley Church if you come back to Little River. Your twins would be in Carter's class, and he's great with that age group," said Lida.

It was an easy thing for them to give each other a quick hug as they parted. "Merry Christmas, Lida," Max said and leaned down again to kiss her cheek. Then, a simple good-bye somehow tumbled into a long embrace. Their kisses were long and loving as their old love in ashes flamed up and drew them into its suddenly familiar warmth. They had no defenses up for a temptation as strong and unexpected as this one. The clock in the distance chimed 5:30.

Max finally pulled away from her and whispered, "Lida, just leave. Now! Please!"

"Oh, Max, I'm so sorry," Lida's gloved hand brushed away tears. "I really apologize."

"Don't, Lida. Please, don't. We're OK," he said as he gripped her arms. "It's not like we planned this. I don't know about you, but I really don't know what happened here."

They said an embarrassed goodbye, and he opened the door of her now very warm car. As she was about to drive away, Max tapped on her window. "Meet me here again before I leave? I could let you know what happens at the hospital. And if you say 'No' we'll both understand."

"You just say when," Lida replied. "I've already planned to make an extra trip back this way to help Mother decorate her tree sometime next week." They agreed on a time to meet at the same coffee shop. The contingency clause was that neither of them was compelled to keep the appointed time if they had second thoughts.

Lida left the parking lot in tears. In her rear view mirror, she could see Max with his head down, his hands jammed in his coat pockets, as he walked over to his rental car. Soon,

Max's car sped around hers in a cloud of snowflakes, and off into the darkness.

They met a few days later as planned, and were able to be surprisingly frank about the re-kindling of their old romance. They knew that they were on dangerous ground, and they carefully probed one another's mind and heart as they walked along the mall for a long time.

"This job offer is almost too good to be true," said Max. "Sally is willing to move, so it looks like this may really happen. But, Li, I will turn it down in a heartbeat if you don't think it is a good idea. I mean, after that goodbye scene last week, maybe it's best if I don't come back?"

Lida didn't hesitate. "I know I don't want to go without seeing you for another twenty years. But, Max, I really do care about my family and about Carter. I don't want to ruin what we have. We've really had to work hard to make this marriage work, but it does work."

"You don't have to ruin anything, Lida," he reassured her. "Sally and the twins mean the world to me, too. You and I seem to have resurrected an old agenda, but it doesn't have to include an affair. As a Christian, I don't want to go against everything I believe in, and I know you don't either. Frankly, I found out the other night that I never stopped loving you; but I'm not willing to let that discovery destroy our families and us. Just promise you'll meet me here once a year or so, and with God's help, that will have to be enough."

"Sort of like 'Same Time Next Year?' " When he looked puzzled, she added, "You know that movie with Alan Alda?"

"Oh, yeah," he then added wryly under his breath, "Don't we wish!" She reached up and touched his jaw as it flexed. He pressed her hand to his cheek, then took it away. Lida realized her palm was wet as she slipped it into her coat pocket.

They spent quite awhile over coffee under the ficus trees. They both knew that it might be a long time before they saw one another again, maybe never if the position at Riverton General didn't work out. Max talked at length about his opportunity. He stopped in the middle of the details and smiled at her, "You know, don't you, Li, that the only thing that has kept me from thinking constantly about you is all the hassle and negotiation around this new position. I'm going to have to find some new mental and emotional boxes for you somewhere inside me."

"Myself, I was thinking of a basket for the total person. And, I'm really sleep deprived! I don't think I have to tell you that I've had the same struggle," replied Lida. They knew that it would take enormous exertion of will power and dedication to their faith for them to maintain their plan. But somehow they did it. A pattern had been set in motion that was to become a steady part of their lives for many years.

Slowly, Riverton General Hospital sweetened the job offer more and more. Not the least of the benefits to Max and his family was moving away from an urban setting and into a small community with a less complicated lifestyle. And, Max would be moving home. He hadn't realized how good that might feel until the chance presented itself.

Max finally accepted the chief surgeon's position. "Dr. Max" and his family became a regular part of his childhood community and church. It was almost like he had never been gone. Even with their different accents, Stefan and Megan fit right into Carter's Sunday School class and the town of Little River.

The two families were often together in social settings, but few people remembered Max and Lida as high school sweethearts. They went through all the family stages in close proximity. Everyone attended games, contests, fundraisers, graduations, showers, and weddings for each other's children. And then the cycle began all over again when the inevitable grandchildren began to arrive. Their lives were loosely entwined and happy.

Still their secret was very alive and very protected. Max and Lida devised a set of signals to communicate with each other: a nod, a wink, a motion, a sound, and a handshake meant the hidden things they could not say. Each reunion at the mall they added another signal to their repertoire. They never compromised the commitments they'd made to their spouses and families. Their contentment was in being together in the community and in their once a year reunion.

The mall visits tapered off when their lives were complicated by aging. First Max, then Lida was alone, but by then Lida's health kept her from driving long distances or from going regularly to church activities. Whenever they did happen to see one another, they easily fell back into their old sign language.

Max suffered a stroke which left him somewhat impaired in his speech and movement, but he was still able to be fairly active. His spirits never flagged. He said he wanted to have his own place, but what he was truly concerned about was being a burden to his children. He chose not to live with either of them, so finally the twins found the best retirement home in the area for him. He took the move to his new surroundings right in his stride, and settled fairly quickly into life in a completely new arena.

A few weeks after Max arrived at the retirement center he made his way down the hall for the evening meal. He was greeted warmly by the people who joined him along the way. With his heart for people and his ready smile, he was already known and accepted in his new neighborhood.

As he turned around from greeting someone near the doorway to the dining room, he nearly knocked over a little lady who was trying quietly to slide behind him without causing any trouble. Obviously a newcomer. He reached out to steady her and was startled to see not a stranger, but Lida. She was a new arrival on the same hallway as Max's.

Although suffering the slow devastation of an arthritic

condition, Lida was mentally alert, but limited in her activities. This second unplanned reunion for Max and Lida was once again one of total surprise. When they saw each other and realized that they were going to be neighbors for the rest of their lives, they both laughed until they cried. At first, the staff was alarmed, but then realized that their tears were from laughter and joy. They kept laughing off and on for several days.

Max and Lida became constant companions. Their best way to communicate was still their old sign language. They were happy together even though they knew that their days were probably numbered. Most of all, they felt that God had given them this reunion as a gift in their old age. Their love story had become bookends that contained all the chapters of their lives.

The family gatherings and parties at the retirement home were perhaps their favorite times. It was easy for the families to plan special occasions together. In fact, the nursing home encouraged them to do this. They could all laugh about old, shared jokes, rehash memories from their church camp nicknamed, "The Lily of the Swamp," and enjoy the bittersweet glow of a few bad times now memories to be joked about. It was pure delight to sit together and enjoy their families. Could this be happening?! Their previous deception now simply added luster to their unique "honeymoon."

Whenever Pastor Wayne from the Lily of the Valley Community Church dropped by on a pastoral call, he was smiling when he left. Max and Lida made him wonder: "Why can't other senior citizens be as positive as those two?"

The staff at the retirement center who caught on to the bond between the two saw to it that they were seated next to each other at various times; the closeness clearly made them happy. They seemed especially pleased to be seated with their afternoon coffee near the twinkle-lit ficus trees in the atrium area.

Max walked with Lida as she moved slowly up and down the halls of their new residence; he knew he needed the activity as well. His condition improved, as did hers, due to their better emotional and physical conditions. However, when Max was not feeling well, Lida could be found by his bedside with her hand resting on his cheek.

Once in awhile Max was teased for winking too much at Lida; or Lida was chided for squeezing Max's hand so hard. They alone knew the wink meant, "I will always love you," and the handshake meant, "Meet me at the mall."

```
┌─────────────────────────────────────────────┐
│ Send To   Attachments                        │
│ ┌───────────────────────────────────────┐ ▲ │
│ │ ⊞📱 LatimerPNG@sopac.org              │ ▒ │
│ │                                       │ ▲ │
│ │                                       │ ▼ │
│ └───────────────────────────────────────┘   │
└─────────────────────────────────────────────┘
```

Subject: Big Brother's Accusations

Attn.: Chuck

No, I am not making up the story about Max Gentry and Lida Sullivan. You know me better than that. Poetic license? Maybe in some of my stories, but not this one. Of course, I did have to fill in some of the blanks etc.

Believe it or not, Rev. Ike told me about Max and Lida. He was one of the few who remembered them as sweethearts in high school. He was in junior high at the time they were in high school. Ike was a big football fan when Max was at his gridiron best.

Recently, I ran into Rev. Ike at a church conference. I mentioned seeing Dr. Max and Lida together out at the retirement center. Ike never would have divulged a word of all this, but I told him how Lida was always winking at Max. He tried, but couldn't keep from laughing....really laughing. Then he said, "I guess the old language is still working." Of course, I had no idea what on earth he was laughing about, and asked him what he meant by "old language."

Before he went on, he asked me not to talk to anyone about what he was going to tell me. He said it was preacher to preacher privileged information, and I agreed. Long story short, when Dr. Max returned to Little River to work for Riverton Hospital, he and Lida met individually with Rev. Ike about their mutual dilemma.

According to him, Max and Lida decided they wanted someone to hold them accountable about their agreement. That's how Rev. Ike learned about their secret.

Later I thought differently about my confidentiality agreement with Rev. Ike. I became uncomfortable knowing about all this without Max and Lida being informed as well. I thought they should know that the secret had been passed on to their new (ahem) cleric. So, on my next visit to the retirement center, I told Dr. Max and Lida that Rev. Ike had told me their secret, but only after I told them about noticing how chummy they had gotten as neighbors. I sure didn't want Rev. Ike to look like he had been talking out of turn.

Max's jaw flexed a few times, and then he said, "Well, who in the world cares what two old people are doing over here at the retirement center anyway?" His blue eyes were really sparkling and he was chuckling by then. He nudged Lida and she said, "I guess it doesn't have to be a secret anymore."

I could tell that they were rather disappointed that the proverbial cat was out of the bag, so I promised to keep it all hush-hush if they wanted me too. But, I also told them that I was going to write a story about them someday, and that their story was definitely going into my storehouse of "good ones." Lida clapped her hands, and said, "Good for you! Let me know if you need anymore details. Be sure to bring me a copy."

So now you know the rest of the story! See, I even have Lida's permission to tell it, but I probably won't be saying much about Max and Lida. It's just too special a relationship for it to be talked about and misunderstood.

Chuck, whatever would I do without my policeman of a brother watching over my every move, as well as every 'jot and tittle' that I write? And, even from cyberspace! For the record, I do try to uphold the standards of truth in journalism. I try not to plagiarize or exaggerate. I do not write for the "National Enquirer." Also, I am pretty sure Jesus wants me to be a truthteller, too. So, you see, I have a bigger motivation than your hot breath sizzling down my neck. And I absolutely promise not to gossip unless it is to convey topics of interest to my totally trustworthy brother.

I'm more worried about you and Laurie learning how to surf than you should be about the faint possibility that I might be fibbing about Dr. Max and Lida! Seriously! Are you sure you ought to be surfing? Aren't there huge waves out there in the Pacific? And, what about sharks? Where did you get surfboards? Don't tell me you are bodysurfing?

I am the designated worrier about this surfing thing. I am definitely not telling the folks you are doing this when you are parents of their grandchildren. And I am their uncle. More lectures will be forthcoming!

Praying for you and yours,
Wayne

P.S. If I come to visit, will you teach me to surf?

LatimerPNG@sopac.org

Subject: Great Vacation

Hi, we're back! The vacation and time away were wonderful. It was great to relax with the kids and not have an agenda, hidden or otherwise. Believe me, the break was much needed and enjoyed. Thanks for your prayers for our ancient van. It definitely rose to the occasion....not one problem along the way.

Looks like everything here at the parsonage survived OK without us. Vic Dabney volunteered for the house-sitting/kitten- feeding job, and he kept everything in good shape.

Our new kitten-from-the-shelter was plenty glad to see us. He went from lap to lap for a day or two as he tried to convince us to never leave him again. On the trip, we came up with a name for him. I told the kids when we brought him home that they could choose his name, but they both had to agree on it. Big Mistake! We've all felt sorry for poor, nameless "Cat Man," as we have been calling him. Cayla wanted him to be "Prince," and Joshua kept insisting on "Raptor." For weeks the battle has been raging!

Finally, we are at the campsite, and Trudy announced it was "Name the Kitten" night. The kids duked it out over the campfire, and with a small measure of compromise, they settled on "Bravo,"... because he is such a brave bunch of no-good fluff. Now it remains to be seen if we can all shift over to the new name. I frankly liked the former title, but Trudy thought the kids needed the experience of working together on something until they reached an agreement. Is she great or what?

We saw all the usual sights around the lake. The kids had never seen a dam, so we wandered around up in that area. One day we rented a boat and explored all those coves and inlets where you and I used to fish and catch nothing. Lots of memories.

We stopped in to see Sam and Nora Loftis. Actually, we had been invited for dinner. We had a super time visiting with them, and ended up bunking in with them overnight. You remember how Nora is about having a bunch of folks around. She still won't take "No" for an answer.

They have done a great job of re-doing their lake cottage for their permanent home. I think they are having a good retirement, but they miss being close to friends in Little River and at church. They have found a little country church out there, but it just isn't the same. I agreed to send them the LOV bulletin and a cassette of the service on a weekly basis. I know, I know. You probably thought you had an exclusive on my sermon tapes, didn't you? Sorry, they also are very hard up for boredom busters.

They are very glad to have Joel, their youngest, living back in the area. He's been staying with them, but is looking for a place to live closer to Little River. Remember how shocked and surprised everyone was when they had a baby so "late in life?" Looks like he has been a joy all along.

We reminisced about a lot of things, and after the kids were asleep, Sheriff Sam shared a dynamite adventure of his. This one will curl your toes for sure. As soon as I write it up, I'll e-mail it over to you.

We went to the resort I told you about for 3 days after leaving the lake. I refuse to tell you how bad my golf game has become, but it was fun to be out on a golf course again. Trudy enjoyed letting the kids roam around and not having to cook. The congregation hit a home run when they gave us this vacation. Sweet people.

On the trip we were wondering, what season are you in down there? What sort of weather do you have this time of year etc.? The concept of another hemisphere is hard for the kids to grasp, so this is a good op to teach them about it.

Trudy and I had a major fight right after we unpacked from the trip. So I think I have some fence mending to do tonight. I don't like to get into it with her, but she can really push all my buttons. I guess I obviously do the same to her. This usually happens when we are tired, which we were. All I said was something about how good it was to get home. Unfortunately for our relationship, I then said something about how much I missed the church and all the fun that goes on over there.

Bam! Things hit the fan over that little remark. She really took it all the wrong way...like the pastorate is more fun and/or important than spending time with her and the kids. Then I made a stupid jab about how she was sounding just like her mother. Not good. I hope the air is clear and we've had one of those great happy endings by the time you read this e-mail.

Thanks for reading this far. Sorry it turned into such an epistle. God only knows how much we miss you and yours.

Love and stuff, Wayne

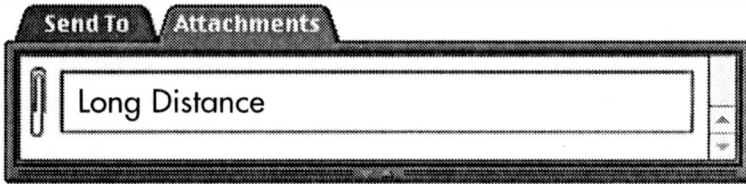

Long Distance

LONG DISTANCE

Jill was radically thankful that school was out. "Funny," she thought, "teachers are as ready for school to be out as the students. Maybe more so." She had straightened her desk, turned in her grades, and left school with relief. Her luggage was already in her car. She wanted to leave town early enough to be able to watch the full moon rise over the lake.

The quiet countryside sped by as she neared the remote lake cabin that had been her childhood haunt for family vacations. She had known that someday she would inherit this small property, but until she actually saw the title in her name, she had not been drawn back. Now, she was anxious to be there.

Jill had called ahead to have distant neighbors, Nora and Sam Loftis, open the cottage and give it a thorough cleaning. The Lily of the Valley Community Church had been the hub of her parents' lives, and Nora and Sam had shared that with them. When Sam took early retirement, they had moved permanently out to their cottage in the hills. Sam had recently been persuaded to take on a rather perfunctory job, Sheriff of Lakeland County.

The Loftises drove in from the lake for her parents' double funeral service. Afterwards, they told Jill that instead of a memorial gift, they would like to clean up the cottage for her when she was ready to use it again. Well, she was ready! It did seem eerie that her parents would not be there, but she brushed away this brief encounter with nostalgia.

The accident that took her parents' lives was now over a

year ago, and she was beginning to feel like her old self. The year, with its grief and sorrow, had been very difficult, but she had recently found herself regaining some of her normal joy in life.

Jill wanted to relax and drop out of sight for a few days. She knew no one would worry about her at work since school was out. Last Sunday at the Lily of the Valley Community Church, she told her co-worker in the Serve the Sheaves Closet Ministry that she would miss her volunteer hours for awhile. "Not to worry! Everyone knows the schedule is crazy in the summer," was the predictable reply.

The Significant Singles Sunday School Class, which she was finding progressively dull, could certainly survive without her. It bothered her that no one shared much of an inner life during the Sunday morning class. Maybe it was because no one had an inner life? Surely, she was not the only one that longed for more than just sharing surface prayer requests and answering the questions in their lesson books? Thankfully, her career brought her in contact with many interesting people and challenging intellectual stimuli. She knew God had placed her on this planet to be a teacher. She loved her job, but most of all, she enjoyed a genuine gift for connecting with children.

However, she knew she needed a break, and it was an exhilarating feeling for her to be suspended from all her responsibilities and relationships. She wondered how long the euphoria would last? She had packed enough correspondence, books, and projects to fight off the specter of boredom. She wanted to catch up on her neglected "Read Through the Bible in a Year" project. This year she was determined to receive her certificate of completion on New Year's Eve at the LOV New Year's party.

Shortly before sunset, she pulled up to Austin's Grocery and Bait Store near the lake cabin. This was an anticipated part of her trip. In her childhood summers, an eagerly awaited adventure was a trip with her mother to Austin's Store for groceries. Candy from the penny candy jars was always on the list of family essentials. She hoped Austin's still had peanut butter logs.

When she walked in and the flimsy screen door with the green chipped paint clattered shut behind her, the past came flooding back. The store was the same. She didn't even have to search for the items she needed. It was somehow comforting to be there, and she lingered over her purchases. She did not forget her penny candy. She wondered how long her 10 peanut butter logs would last?

As she pushed the rickety grocery cart up to the counter, the elderly clerk wiped his nicotine stained fingers on his shabby apron as he recognized her.

"Aren't you the Sinclairs' girl?"

"Yes, I'm Jill. I didn't know if I'd see a familiar face here or not. How are you, Mr. Austin?"

"Well, I'm a lot older, but I'm fine. Things haven't changed much. Most of our young folks move away, so just a few of us are left to hold down what is left of Lakeland County."

Jill smiled. "I guess I'm one who's coming back, at least for a little while."

"I s'pose that cottage is yours now, huh? I was mighty sorry to hear about your parents' accident."

"Thanks, Mr. Austin. I guess they never knew what hit them." She paid her bill and Mr. Austin put her belongings in the grocery bags she had remembered to bring along. This early re-cycling habit was born long ago out of necessity. She could remember her mother saying, "Don't let me forget the grocery bags I've been saving for Mr. Austin."

Mr. Austin cleared his throat and asked, "How long you planning on staying, girlie?"

"I'm not sure yet. I've bought food for 4 or 5 days, so I'll stay at least that long, maybe a little longer."

Mr. Austin was making her impatient with his questions as he slowly put her bags in a discarded cardboard box. He still had the same musty odor about him that she remembered from her childhood. She wondered if he ever changed his clothes.

"Well, come see us again."

"I will, I will," she said impatiently as she picked up the box. She was glad to get away from her unexpected inquisition.

She shoved open the old screen door with her toe, and struggled out with her groceries. A truck pulled in beside her car, and she had to wait to back out. She recognized the driver as the son of the Rayburns who owned the only other cottage on this part of the lake.

Jill knew Mr. Austin would take great delight in telling the Rayburns' son, she thought his name was Jeff, all about her arrival. She also predicted he would embellish the tale with an exaggerated account of her parents' accident, and top it off with exactly what she had bought at his store. Jill smiled. She was not usually a subject of local gossip. As a twenty-nine year old, single schoolteacher, and with her simple hairstyle and tailored clothing, she rarely stirred things up enough to interest the gossips. She was always surprised when someone told her she had beautiful skin or lovely gray eyes. A quick look in the mirror usually confirmed her thoughts that nothing had changed.

The cottage looked remarkably serene in the summer shadows of evening. A light was on over the dining room table, so she knew that Sam and Nora had cleaned up the cabin as they had promised. She quickly unloaded her luggage and food, then watched the darkness deepen as she sat on the screened porch overlooking the lake.

"This is what I've been missing," she said out loud. As the tree frogs began their nightly chorus, she found herself suddenly nostalgic about the many nights in her childhood that she went to sleep listening to their song. She saw a light come on eventually at the Rayburns' place in the distance. Probably Jeff lived there now. She wondered how he made a living up here in the hills.

Jill's vacation, simply stated, was a success. The days ran into each other, and she found herself reluctant to go home. So she stayed. The thought of her tiny apartment in Little River was stifling. Instead, she found lazy satisfaction in roaming the woods. She collected woodsy things, and found several new insect specimens for her classroom.

Most of all, she enjoyed floating out on the lake on a plastic raft she had found while rummaging in the hall closet. She knew she was not supposed to swim alone, but she was a strong swimmer, and never swam out far from the redwood pier and her cottage. It pleased her to think of it that way…"my cottage."

The classroom, much as she loved being a teacher, seemed a million miles away, and the only other sign of civilization on her planet was the distant light at the other end of the lake every evening. She went back to Mr. Austin's store for more supplies, and had another grilling from the old gentleman. She felt like he knew all about her by now. He had gone down a long list of questions that pried into her life and even checked out if she had a sweetheart back in the city. She was tired of people asking about her social life that had been non-existent for sometime now. She wasn't sure if she was a blessing, but she did know for certain that she was officially "unclaimed."

Once she felt lonesome, and drove over to visit with Sam and Nora. She wanted to personally thank them for cleaning up the lake cottage for her. They asked her to stay and have dinner with them, and then watch the sunset from their deck. It was delightful to see them, but not an experience she rushed to duplicate. She knew she should invite them over to her place, but she never got around to it.

Three weeks into Jill's escape from reality, she began to think about returning home. She was finished with her cache of books, and she had caught up on her correspondence, Bible reading program, and several craft projects. She felt rested mentally and physically.

Jill carefully planned for her last day. She would pack almost everything the evening before, and spend the last day doing her favorite things: hiking, sitting on the porch, and swimming.

Her last hike was spectacular. The breeze was in her face, and the old path that followed the lakeshore took her quickly along the scenic route. On days like this, she felt like she could reach out and touch the mountains across the lake. By the time she reached home, she was ready for lunch and the hammock on the front porch. She dozed awhile, and was awakened by the telephone. Nora Loftis was on the other end of the line telling her to remember that part of their deal with her included cleaning and locking up the cabin for her. She knew her parents would be pleased that Sam and Nora had taken such good care of her.

She saved the swim for her last big event. She loved the clear water and the sense of being buoyed along on liquid silver. As she floated, she thought about her life, and where God might lead her now that her parents were so suddenly gone. She stretched out face down on her float, and began to think about paddling back toward the pier and traveling back to Little River.

Jill never saw a slight ripple in the water, nor the dark form swim up underneath her. She was thrown into the water, and dragged under. Her face was allowed to come to the surface under the floating mat that was now moving rapidly toward the shore. Whenever she struggled or cried out, she was quickly submerged again. Whoever had grabbed her was incredibly strong, but did not intend to drown her. Once Jill realized this, she tried to figure out what was happening.

"What on earth is going on? Who is this? Why does anyone want to do this to me?" These were just a few of the questions whirling simultaneously through Jill's mind. She was aware of being in the grip of a very strong person in complete scuba gear, and she could see enough to tell that they were coming closer to the lakeshore.

Just before they left the water, she felt the sharp jab of a needle in her hip. In seconds, she was beginning to go limp in the diver's grip. She roused briefly as she was being dragged into a waiting truck. She struggled weakly as she was bound and gagged by the driver who had by now shed his scuba gear. She recognized him. It was Jeff Rayburn. Jill sensed the truck was moving before she lost consciousness.

Jill's mind awoke before her body. It took her a few moments to piece together what had happened. She remembered being thrown off her raft, dragged to the shoreline, then feeling the hypodermic needle. Now she had to figure out where she was and what was happening to her.

As she tried to think coherently, she kept drifting in and out of her drug induced stupor. She slowly became aware of things happening around her. She registered several realities: she was completely prone and she was almost sure that her swimsuit had been removed. She was restrained, blindfolded, and gagged. She was not alone. She could hear rhythmic and unfamiliar voices. Though blindfolded, she could dimly see flickering lights, so she knew it was nighttime. She wondered what time it was, and how long she had been unconscious.

Jill felt like a pawn in an unfamiliar game. She was beginning to realize that whatever the game, she was a major part of it. But what would the next move be?

Voices moved closer to her. One voice she knew. Mr. Austin spoke secretively,

"Well, you done a good job, Jeff."

"Maybe," whispered Jeff in return. "I hope I didn't do all this on a fluke. This isn't my idea of fun, you know. How come you're so sure she's a virgin? "

"You kin take my word for it, son. When you've been around as long as I have, you kin jest tell. Anyhow, she all but told me herself one day in the store. But, look here, Jeff, who's going to know the difference anyhow? They'll believe whatever I tell them."

"Look, Mr. Austin, could you give me my money now? I don't want to wait around. I need to get on home."

"We don't pass the hat for the collection until after the initiation ceremony, so you'll just have to hold yer horses."

Jill was trying to piece together this new information. "I'm a virgin. OK. I'm at a meeting. Somehow Jeff Rayburn and Mr. Austin are up to something. But how do I fit into this puzzle?" All the while, the chanting, the flickering lights, the brutish atmosphere established by Jeff and Mr. Austin never changed. Terror kept rushing at Jill, but she was able to pray, and to keep juggling the information that was coming at her.

She could hear more voices. The number of the voices increased and made her know that a crowd was gathering. She could feel a breeze, so she decided that she must be outside. Now she was sure that she was not covered. She began to shiver.

"Hey, she moved! Where is everyone? It's time to start!"

"Go get Old Man Austin," she heard a raspy voice demand.

"He's gone to get the initiate," a woman replied.

"Well, he'd better hurry. I think she's coming around. He may need to give her some more of that 'joy juice' that Jeff used," the raspy voice continued. Several people laughed.

More chants! More flickering lights! By now, Jill was completely awake. There was some sort of meeting going on, and she was on display for that meeting. Her sense of modesty revolted, and she squirmed just enough to find out that she was very securely tied down

Jill began to silently pray. Her prayers were confused, but she knew that God could make sense of them. Thankfully, she was suddenly surrounded by a peaceful sense of His presence. It almost felt like a blanket had been thrown over her shivering body.

A new sound began. It was the sound of metal being drawn across a stone. A blade was being sharpened. Her prayers quickly became more specific.

"God! Are they going to use that knife on something? On me? Lord, please protect me." But then she remembered the calm of His presence from moments before. She calmed down inside, and was surprised to realize that imminent death did not frighten her as much as she thought it would. Torture was another matter.

The chanting voices became louder and louder. Jill wondered if maybe this were a Ku Klux Klan meeting. If so, why was she here? She'd certainly had no dealings with race issues or politics. Little River had never experienced bigotry of any form that she knew of.

Maybe this was a religious cult of some sort? Was it pagan or Christian? But again, why was she here? The atmosphere was definitely not Christian, and no cult she was aware of put naked women on display.

She could hear Mr. Austin coming back. She remembered now being uncomfortable when he grilled her about the details of her life. Was he the key to all this? How could an old grocer be part of something so sinister? On and on her mind spun.

There was a thought lurking just below the surface of her mind. She kept going back to it. It was the memory of a conversation. The memory had something to do with the screened door with the chipped green paint at Austin's Grocery and Bait Store. Finally, the memory roared out of her subconscious.

Jill had been eating her penny candy and waiting inside the old screen door while her mother paid for the groceries. Outside, two rather slovenly women were talking about a midnight meeting at the old pavilion out by the lake. Later, when Jill asked her mother about what she had heard, she was told, "I've heard that there are people back in the hills who worship the devil. They have secret midnight meetings." When Jill had asked more about why anyone would worship the devil, her mother said it was too scary and changed the subject.

The reality hit Jill head-on. This was one of those secret meetings where people in the hills worship Satan. This is what her mother didn't want to tell her about because it might scare her. Her mother was right. Jill was terrified. The full realization of what was happening became more clear to her as the conversations around her droned on.

The initiate was being summoned. The knife was still being sharpened. The chanting was increasing. Then she overheard some more comments by Mr. Austin as he talked with the candidate.

"You ready, son?"

"Yes, sir, I am."

"You know this will raise our group way up in the hierarchy of our brotherhood, don't you? You are very privileged to be chosen for this part of the ceremony. "

"I know. I am very grateful for this privilege. All this means a lot to me."

"Do you know what to do?"

"Yes, sir. I do. After the ceremonial stuff is done, you give a speech and I give my response."

"Right, and then?"

"I guess I just wait for your signal."

"That's right. When I hand you the knife, you go for the mark that I'm going to make right now."

Jill felt the cool ink and smelled the marker as it touched

the skin over her heart. It was all she could do to keep her body from recoiling along with her mind and soul.

"God! No! No!" She screamed in silent prayer. She knew tears were soaking into her blindfold by now. Her Bible reading program had just been about how the Israelites had been drawn into human sacrifice and the worship of false gods. She had a deep revulsion when she realized that tonight she was to be the sacrifice in some sort of a pagan rite.

"God of heaven! Do not let them use me to worship Satan. Protect me from the evil one as you have promised. Save me from this, Lord!" On and on her prayer went, not just for her own safety, but for deliverance from honoring Satan.

~~

The phone rang at the Loftis residence as Sam was brushing his teeth. Nora called to him, and said it sounded like a long distance call. When he reached the phone, he could barely hear for all the static.

"What's that?" he shouted. "Yes, this is Sam Loftis. You'll have to speak up. Really bad connection here."

There was a long silence as Nora stood by with a curious tilt to her head.

"You want me to what?" bellowed Sam. "Yes, I'm the sheriff! That doesn't mean I can go all over creation on some wild goose chase in the middle of the night." More static, and more silence.

"Aw'right, I'll listen to what you have to say. Make it snappy," Sam decided that the man on the other end might really need some help.

He covered the phone with his hand, and kept Nora informed as the conversation went on. "This guy says there is trouble up at the pavilion. He wants me to round up some men and go up there." By now, Nora's eyes were as big as saucers.

"Look, mister, how do I know this is for real?"

Silence, then, "Yes, I know Jill." The look of concern was deepening on Sam's face. "No way would that girl be at a satanic meeting."

Nora was horrified. She ran to pick up the other extension. The man and the static continued: "Just go up there and help her. Take some men with you, and take some heat so these people will know you are serious."

"Heat?" Sam asked in a blank sort of way.

"Yes, Sam. You know, fire power! As in 'guns'!" The man was very irritated. "How can you be a sheriff and not be prepared to help someone? Look, I doubt anyone will get violent. Once they are discovered, everyone will just scatter."

Nora now covered her end of the line, "We have to do something, Sam," she pleaded.

"Oh, all right," said Sam as he slammed down his toothbrush and reached for a pen. He sputtered something about how was he supposed to know that "heat" meant guns.

"Just one thing, I'm not moving on this until you give me your name."

After a long silence, the voice at the other end said, "Michael."

"That's it! Just Michael? Look, fella, there are lots of Michaels out there. You gotta give me more than that," shouted Sam over the static.

"That's it. That's my name. Michael. Sam, you've always been stubborn. Nora, talk some sense into this guy. Please! Now move. Hurry!"

The line went dead, and Sam stared at the phone. He didn't have time to figure it all out, but whoever this Michael was must know both himself and Nora, and Jill. He decided to worry about it later. Within a few minutes, Sam had grabbed his shotgun and was putting on his jacket. He jotted down some names for Nora.

"Call these men; they live on the way up to the pavilion. Tell them to fall in behind me when I come by. You'd better tell them to bring their guns, but they're not to load them up unless I give the word."

"Don't you want Joel to go with you? I'll go wake him up," volunteered Nora.

"Nope. Remember, he has his first meeting over at the school tomorrow with his coaching staff before they leave for the summer. If I need him, I'll call you on my cell."

Sam was gone; but, before he pulled out of the driveway, he stopped long enough to put the plastic bubble with the suction cup on top of his pickup. His children had given it to him as a joke when he became sheriff of Lakeland County. The red light was whirling before he drove away.

Nora began enlisting a posse and praying.

The neighbors' vehicles fell in behind Sam's pickup, and they wound their way up the hill to the pavilion. Sam was thinking that Nora must've done a good job of convincing them to cooperate with Michael. Who in the world was he anyway?

The men parked down the hill from the pavilion. No one slammed a door or made a sound. Sam explained in whispers what was going on. They moved out in the darkness and stationed themselves at intervals around the pavilion. They waited for Sam's low whistle. They were to approach the meeting with their unloaded guns in full view across their chests. All the chanting of the ceremony and the flickering torches gave them ample coverage as they stood at their posts.

The whistle came during Mr. Austin's speech. The rough-hewn posse moved out in unison. Some of them had heard the rumors of satanic meetings, but no one had any doubts about what they were dealing with by the time they walked into the ring of torches, heard the chanting, and saw Jill. The knife beside her on the table glistened in the light of the torches.

Sam's rough shout and authoritative swagger, which he had just acquired moments before, caught the worshippers off guard.

"Everybody listen up! Quiet! I'm Sheriff Sam Loftis, and I have a group of fine gentlemen from Lakeland County here with me. Everyone remains here in the pavilion, and no one gets hurt. Mr. Austin, you step up here beside me, and I want you to invite anyone else you think ought to go downtown with us. Otherwise, I'm holding you personally responsible for this whole damn shindig. I want my men to confiscate the materials around here, and take down everyone's name. Someone take that knife and cut Jill loose."

Sam moved quickly to cover Jill with his jacket. Mr. Austin, with a vice-like grip on Jeff Rayburn's wrist, stood with his head down. Everyone could hear Jeff cursing the old man for holding onto him. He kept saying he didn't belong to this group. But Jill composed herself long enough to identify him as the one who had brought her up here, so Jeff's innocence didn't last very long.

The makeshift posse moved swiftly to break up the meeting and carry out Sam's orders. Michael, whoever he was, had been right about how the crowd would vanish without any violence. One of Sam's men gave Jill a heavy blanket and a cup of coffee from his thermos.

~~

When Jill and Sam were in the safety of the truck, Jill dissolved into sobs. She had held on to her emotions as long as possible. Oddly, feeling safe again was more than she could handle. Sam told her to take as long as she needed to calm down, that he wasn't in any hurry. He also assured her that no one was going to hurt her again. He found some unused paper napkins in the glove compartment and handed them to her to wipe her tears. Slowly, she was able to settle herself down. She tried to make a feeble joke or two, but Sam assured her that this was nothing to laugh about. She readily agreed.

Eventually, he started the truck and rolled down to the main road. As Sam drove with Jill back down the mountain toward the Loftis cabin, he abruptly asked her, "Jill, you got a boyfriend named Michael?"

"No way, Sam! You know I don't have a boyfriend at all," Jill stammered. She was still shaking, but was beginning to warm up under the blanket that had been wrapped around her. Sam went on to tell her about the mysterious phone call that had rallied the posse for her rescue. They discussed the whole experience with puzzled voices. Soon they were pulling into the driveway and Nora was on the porch waving to them.

As Jill stepped out of the truck, she said to Sam, "Whatever we're dealing with, thanks for taking that call seriously. I think I know how Isaac felt, although you don't look much like a ram in the bush, Sam."

"Oh, here," Sam said as he pulled Jill's swimsuit out of the pocket of his jacket.

"I probably won't ever wear this one again, Sam. But thanks,....thank you for everything." Jill pulled the blanket around the mark over her heart as Sam walked with her toward the waiting warmth and security of the Loftis cabin. Nora was running towards her with arms outstretched and all sorts of concern.

"Jill, honey! Look at you! What on earth was going on up at the pavilion?"

Sam let go of Jill only after Nora took over. "You're in good hands now, Jill. But, I'm warning you, she'll want to know every detail. I'm going to follow the other men down to the jail with Mr. Austin and Jeff. I reckon the state trooper will be out first thing in the morning to talk to you. He'll want to know about this long distance call, so I guess we'll just tell him how much we don't know."

"Nora, take a picture before you two scrub that mark off. That'll be evidence. And you'd better wake up Joel. Send him over to the Sinclair cottage to check it out. Tell him to stick around awhile to be sure trouble doesn't show up over there, and then lock it up tight before he leaves. Be sure he takes some 'heat,' " he winked at Nora. "Don't wait up."

Nora saluted the Sheriff of Lakeland County as he drove off with the red light on top of his truck still whirling round and round.

Send To ⟍ Attachments

LatimerPNG@sopac.org

Subject: Hellooooo?

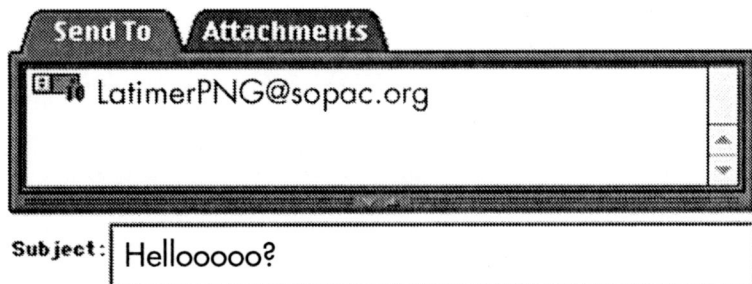

We haven't heard from you in awhile, but by now I'm used to your abuse. Also, I realize that you are busy-busy. So don't sweat it. I do know that no news is good news.

All's well here....mostly. We're in the midst of everything. I never knew there could be so many committees, and they all want me to be on them. They don't seem to get the idea that they can run things with their own talents/gifts without my continual presence. I guess things are going well. At least it seems that way to me. I get some complaints about my sermons being too long when there is something on TV sports that starts at noon on Sunday.

Strange. . . I work so hard to fill up those minutes. Seems like they would want to get their money's worth and hear a whole lot of stuff on Sunday. After all, they are paying me to preach, aren't they?

Speaking of strange, I have a couple mind bogglers to share with you. Title this true story "Financial Difficulty." This is one I'm not very proud of. I'm reluctant to divulge this info; however, it is something that I am really struggling with and need your prayers about. And, anyway it is no secret anymore.

So here goes,
Wayne

```
┌─ Send To ─┬─ Attachments ─┐
│                            │
│  ▌ Financial Difficulty    │ ▲
│                            │ ▼
└────────────────────────────┘
```

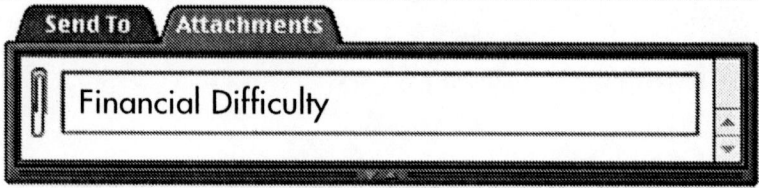

FINANCIAL DIFFICULTY

Rev. Ike has been indicted for white-collar crime. When he left the ministry here, he changed careers and went into a financial consulting firm. Remember, he'd been doing this sort of thing on the side while he was pastor here? At that time, they needed extra income to help with their children's college expenses. When he left the Lily of the Valley Church, we heard that he had taken a full time job in the consulting firm, and how happy he was.

Ike became a specialist in assisting elderly people with retirement plans and investments. He made out plans for a lot of the LOV church members before he left town. It turns out that he took in their funds, but never made the investments. They would get notices from him that all was well and had been invested, but never received any documents or statements from the financial institutions. Finally, some of them compared notes and blew the whistle on him.

Ike and I have visited briefly on the phone, and it is like talking to a stranger. I thought I knew him pretty well since he was our pastor for those years that I was in seminary. It was always good to talk "preacher talk" with him whenever we'd come home to visit the folks. He had such a solid ministry here, or so we thought.

Hold on, there's more to the story.....

Our board decided to review the financial records from the years that Ike was here, and some big time questions have evolved from their investigation. Apparently Ike and Trevor Langley, the man who was the church treasurer then, had a big confrontation in private. A sizeable chunk of money was missing from the church account, but Ike 'fessed up and returned most of the funds that were missing. Langley agreed to cover for him since Ike was making up the deficit. When Ike left LOV, they agreed to let bygones be bygones. At that time, Ike promised Trevor he would send in the rest of the money as soon as he received his first paycheck at his new job. But the money is still missing.

Now Trevor feels totally betrayed and is covered over with shame. Of course, he divulged everything when all this hit the fan. Poor guy, he thought he was helping Ike get through some rough times financially. So he was totally blind-sided when this whole thing came to light.

As you can tell, I'm caught right in the middle of this, and feel way over my head. So pray for me a bunch. I have lost lots of sleep over this mess. Anyway, I'm wiped. Any advice for me, brother?

I guess in this case, the shepherd is the one lost in the wilderness. How can a minister of the gospel consciously compromise himself like this? The sad part is, we know most of the people involved. Several couples have lost their entire retirement package with no way to retrieve it. These dear folks trusted Ike, had known him for years, and are heartsick over his betrayal. He was their former pastor, so of course they thought they could trust him.

The second strange twist has to do with Vic Dabney and some more of the story about his daughter, Jenny. It is really amazing how these dear people struggle to keep their family intact. I'll e-mail it on over later. You and Laurie will love this Raleigh. I'm glad that I arrived here as pastor in time to be a part of their story.

Yours,
Wayne

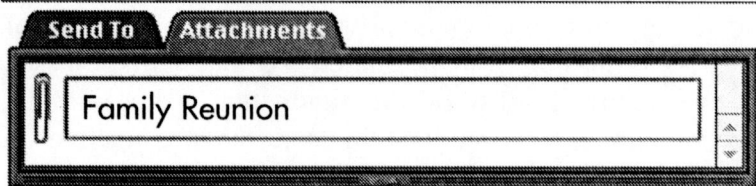

FAMILY REUNION

I

When Zachary was three months old, Vic and Stella decided to take a vacation with Darcy over spring break. The Day Care Corral was closed for the vacation, which gave Jenny a chance to relax at home with Chelsea and Zachary. She had been invited to go along on the trip with the rest of the family, but she declined. A road trip with two little children would change the vacation for everyone. She knew that all six of them needed some space.

On this afternoon, she'd been busy inside and out, both cleaning out drawers and planting new spring bedding plants. One of Chelsea's friends had called her to come over to play, but she would be back home any minute. Jenny had finally gone inside and was preparing a quick meal for the two of them when the doorbell rang.

She could see a strange blue Trans-Am in the driveway, and decided this must be the delivery of some overdue supplies for the Day Care Corral. She'd left instructions for deliveries to come to the house over the spring break. She opened the door with Zachary in her arms. There stood a tall army officer in full-dress uniform. It was Raleigh Lawrence.

"Hi, Jenny. I hope you don't mind my dropping by like this?"

She heard herself say, "No, it's OK," as she stepped outside onto the front porch.

Raleigh went on. "I'm on my same leave schedule as last

year, and thought I'd at least stop by and apologize for not ever calling you." He paused and cleared his throat, "I know I'm taking a real chance here."

"Oh," gulped Jenny.

"Well, Jason took off and didn't leave any way to reach him, and I lost your address and phone number. So, here I am again. Remember my cousin, Dee Wight Smith, the one who works over at Slocum Prison? I'm going to spend the rest of my leave over at his place, then travel on to Cleveland for a special detail in management. After that, I'll have another short break before going over to Europe for a two year tour of duty."

"Oh," she said again.

"I guess I wanted to show off this uniform to somebody. I just graduated from officers' training school. Drum-roll, please!" He made a turn around and snapped his fingers so that Jenny could get the full effect of his accomplishment.

"That's nice," Jenny responded with a bit of a smile. At this point, Raleigh felt like this acknowledgement on Jenny's part was almost a standing ovation.

"You baby-sit this little guy these days?" He reached over and wiggled Zachary's toes. He was beginning to feel very uncomfortable since he was getting so little conversation back from Jenny. He had about exhausted his supply of opening remarks.

"Oh, it seems like he's here a lot." She stepped back.

"Well, I guess you can't go out to dinner with me since you're tied up here?"

"Probably not tonight, Raleigh. But Chelsea, you remember my daughter, will be home in a few minutes, and I was just cooking us some dinner. If you don't mind taking your chances with Spaghetti-O's you're welcome to eat with us." She had intended to get rid of him, and now she couldn't believe she'd just asked this man in for dinner.

"Well, OK, Jenny, thanks! I hope you're serious? That's

the best offer I've had in several months. Any meal in a home with a kitchen sounds terrific to me." He was quick to accept, and quite pleased.

"Well, then, come in. I'll get things on the table," Jenny replied quietly. Raleigh followed her into the house.

"Let me take that cowboy off your hands while you do your kitchen thing. What's his name?"

"This is Zachary. You sure you don't mind? He can be a handful when he's hungry, which he usually is. But, I probably need to change his diaper before I hand him over."

"No problem. Let me have his diaper. I'm an old hand at this tour of duty."

He put Zachary down on the couch while Jenny ran for a diaper. She didn't want to send Raleigh back to the nursery. He might see that Zachary was more than just a baby-sitting job for her. When she returned, Raleigh had Zachary's overalls off and was ready for the diaper. It was obvious that he knew how to handle a baby.

"So, how come you know how to do diapers so well?" she asked.

"I guess I didn't tell you last year that I'm an older brother to five other kids. My mother and I raised them all after my father was killed in an industrial accident. My baby brother was still in diapers when that happened. So I learned early on how to do a lot of things most teenagers get to skip."

"OK, but I'm warning you, keep that fancy uniform out of his range." Raleigh gave her a grin and a mock salute.

After Zachary was all cleaned up, Raleigh played awhile with him. Jenny could hardly cook for staring at the two of them together. He took off his dress jacket and tie, and offered to help her set the table. As they moved around the kitchen, their conversation was light, and mostly about his past year's experiences. Jenny was very guarded. Chelsea came home, and they all enjoyed Jenny's very simple, but delicious meal.

"That was good, Jenny," said Raleigh, "but are we having those Spaghetti-O's you promised me for dessert?"

"No, you're lucky! I made what I think you army men would call a 'mid-course correction.' I decided to save Spaghetti-O's for another time. But there's some of my mom's apple pie if you're still hungry for some dessert?"

" 'Still' is a very flexible word when it comes to my appetite, Jenny. How about it, Chelsea? Do you think we should polish off your granny's apple pie? Please, say 'yes!' "

"Sure," said Chelsea. "But save some for my brother and me." And she ran out the back door to play some more before it got dark.

Jenny cringed inwardly, and hoped that Raleigh missed Chelsea's remark. Why did she have to say that anyway? She knew Zachary couldn't eat apple pie! They cleared off the dinner plates, and Jenny dished up the apple pie. She put on a pot of coffee to go with it. There was a long silence.

Finally, Raleigh spoke up in a clipped voice, "So Zachary is Chelsea's brother, Jenny?"

Jenny nodded and did not look up from her hands, which trembled slightly as she poured their coffee.

"Cream and sugar?" she asked.

"Both, please." He took a sip of hot coffee as she handed him his cup and continued, "Then, I guess I may have a hunch why you let this little guy pass as a baby-sitting job." Jenny did not reply but began to bite her bottom lip. There was another long silence as Raleigh stood with his arms folded and looked out the kitchen window at Chelsea on her swing set.

"Look here, Jenny. I definitely remember what happened on our blind date, and I came by to sort of clear that up if I could. I feel like a real jerk that I didn't stay in touch. But I can count, Jenny,....add and subtract. And I can see, too, Jenny. I can see that Zachary is about 3 months old, and that he's mixed. His color is different from Chelsea's, a lot different."

Jenny tried to look calm. But she was unable to speak. After a short break to catch his breath, Raleigh went on.

"Am I making sense? Am I on the right track here, Jenny?" His voice was full of emotion as he looked down at her, his arms still folded. "Talk to me!"

"You're right on target, Lieutenant. You're very perceptive," she answered in a choked whisper. She tried to look at him, but by now her eyes were brimming over with tears.

"My God, Jenny! Don't be messing with me now. I came over here to see if you would even speak to me, and to tell you I'm usually not a one-night-stand kind of a guy. And, Bingo! I find out I'm a father?" His face contorted with the emotions that rushed over him. He pressed one hand hard on his eyelids as he braced himself on the kitchen counter with the other. Every muscle in his body was tense.

Still tongue-tied, Jenny gingerly covered his hand on the counter with hers. Finally, she said, "Raleigh, I'll tell you anything you want to know. I'm sorry you had to find out about your son this way. There aren't any secrets. I just didn't know what to say when you first asked me about Zachary out on the porch."

Now, Raleigh was the one who was speechless. He kept looking down and kicking at the base of the kitchen counter with his shiny, spit and polish toe. Jennifer went on.

"When you never called or wrote, I guess I assumed you had vanished forever, and all of a sudden, here you are." She was openly crying now. "I'm wiped out, too, Raleigh."

"OK, all right," said Raleigh as he began to calm down. Now he was leaning over Zachary in his infantseat, looking at him and shaking his head in wonder. "Mmm-mmh," was the only sound he made for awhile. Zachary was looking into his father's eyes and cooing like this was an everyday event. Finally, Jenny spoke.

"Let's take our dessert, and go outside on Dad's porch.

We can keep an eye on Chelsea, and we can talk about all this." She picked up the plates, and Raleigh picked up Zachary who was just about to nod off to sleep.

As they were going out the door, Raleigh said, "Wow, look out there, Zach! Don't miss the sunset God painted just for us tonight. He's sure bad with a paint brush."

When Jenny went back inside for their coffee cups, she took a minute to dry her eyes, and to get her emotions and feelings under control. She was trying to balance being afraid but calm at the same time. Her Dad's porch seemed like an appropriate place to find out how Raleigh's discovery and her feelings fit together.

II.

The rest of the evening was filled with putting children to bed, and a long, long conversation. Jenny learned that Raleigh, true to his word, was honestly not one to mess around with girls on a first date. They had both been caught up in a powerful attraction that was attached to a deep need in Jenny's turmoil, and an unexpected commitment on Raleigh's part.

It was the tug of this feeling that he had been trying to shake for the past twelve months. He dated other girls, tried not dating at all, but could not forget his blind date in Little River. Jenny had to laugh as he told her about how scared he was to ring the Dabneys' doorbell, and how hard he had worked on his uniform to be sure to impress her.

Jenny's story was about her struggle with being pregnant and how her parents had helped her out and supported her. She did not spare the details of her dilemma, nor the anger that she and her family had faced about this man who didn't care enough to stay in touch.

"I'm glad my parents aren't here tonight so just the two

of us can talk about this. I doubt my dad would've let you in the door. But, Raleigh, without their support, I'm pretty sure I wouldn't have kept this baby. Back then, I was pretty desperate. Now I can't imagine life without Zachary."

Later, they were outside again, sitting on the steps of Vic's porch, and each leaning against opposite posts. Raleigh was very aware that Jenny was keeping her distance from him, and he supposed that was understandable. He was just now beginning to absorb what she had gone through. She and her family had been through a horrendous struggle, while he, on the other hand, was merely off dreaming about their first date. His biggest struggle had been trying to decide whether or not to try to find her again.

Raleigh explained his side of the past year. "I didn't think that I would have much of a chance here, Jenny. Any long-term relationship seemed out of the question. I don't know why, but the racial thing seemed like a big hurdle to me. I guess that's why I left and didn't call back. It was really more than not having your phone number." Raleigh's admission of his fears about their different cultures moved their discussion to a much deeper level.

Jenny picked up with her side of the story. "I know about the cultural thing, too. I know exactly what you are talking about. It's called prejudice. I've learned a lot about our world, and how cruel it can be, Raleigh. But, I've also learned that there are a lot of decent people out there. Some of them have tried their best to help ease Zachary and me back into the mainstream of this town."

There was a pause in their conversation, and Jenny asked, "So, why did you really show up tonight?" They both knew the unspoken accusation that she had thrown down between them. Was Raleigh Lawrence there for another date just like their other one?

"It's not what you're thinking! I keep telling you. You just wouldn't go away, Jenny. Give yourself credit for nearly driving me nuts. I finally decided that I owed it to you, but also to myself to find you again.

"But let me back up a little. The final push on this came when I was in OCS and out in the field. My best buddy is a brother from Georgia who's married to a hispanic girl from Texas. They've struggled a lot to put their cultures together. They have found out that the Army is a pretty accepting place for a mixed couple." He squirmed and hesitated.

"Well, go on," said Jenny.

"I'm going as fast as I can here, girl," he whistled and continued. "About a month ago, we were directing training maneuvers, and spent all night outside. We were huddled under this plastic tarp. The weather was terrible. One of those late winter ice storms was in full sway, and not much was happening. We were super bored, and got to talking. The topic of bi-racial dating came up. We couldn't go any-where, so I decided to spill my questions and frustrations about this pretty white girl named Jenny. I laid it all out for him. All about our blind date. Everything."

"By the middle of the wee small hours, he had the whole story. By dawn he had bet me $100 that I wouldn't have the guts to go find you again. He really gave me a hard time for not doing anything about staying in touch with you. His con-tention is that the bi-racial relationship dilemma is a thing of the past. Of course, the small detail of a Zachary never entered my mind."

Finally, they were too emotionally exhausted to be coher-ent. "I hope you don't mind if I come back in the morning. I think we still have lots more to talk about, and my furlough is looking shorter all the time. But before I leave," Raleigh patted his heart, "Could I go in and see Zach one more time?"

She couldn't refuse a father's request, could she? Raleigh went in to the little nursery corner, picked up Zachary, and held him close for a few minutes.

"Why don't you bring him out with us? He's probably going to want to eat pretty soon anyhow," suggested Jenny. They walked out to the blue Trans-Am. The evening was lush with scents of spring, and lightning fired up the hills in the distance.

Jenny asked, "Would you mind if Pastor Wayne, the new minister from our church, stops by here tomorrow? My church family has helped me so much, and I would really like for you to meet him."

"Jenny, I'll meet anyone who's been good to you and Zach. I know you didn't make it through this on your own. You have really done a great job. Zach has a super mom." He smiled and gave Zachary back to her.

He opened the door to get into his car. Then he turned back and laughed self-consciously. "You know what? Something just dawned on me. My brother from Georgia owes me $100. But there's more."

"What?" asked Jenny.

"He'll never believe me if I take off without kissing you good night. And, besides, I don't think I want to leave unless I do." He took Zachary's hand and asked his son, "Zach, my man, wake up and tell this lady she can trust me. So?" he shrugged and opened his arms.

She didn't object as he wrapped himself around both of them. He kissed Zachary and then her. "This time, Jenny, I'll be back. I promise!" he whispered. In his heart, he was singing the "Doxology."

He started his car and lowered the window. "I'm on with Dee Wight to shoot some hoops in the morning. Then, I'll come on over here. I'll bring lunch, so don't even think about feeding us those Spaghetti-O's you're saving."

As Lt. Lawrence drove out of the driveway, he turned up the bass on his car stereo so the neighborhood could feel his departure. He grinned and waved. In his rearview mirror he could see Jenny wagging her finger at him.

Send To	Attachments

LatimerPNG@sopac.org

Subject: Ms. Demarco

Hi. No big news. I just put Cayla and Joshua in time-out for coming to blows over which TV program to watch. Ah, fatherhood! Now I'm watching the big tennis tournament for a few minutes. I'll also try to write to you.

Remember, I was going out to visit Ms. Demarco awhile back? Well, after one of her incredible lattes with a piece of her lemon pie, I was trying to make small talk. So I asked her if she'd ever been married.

She said " Well, not too many folks here in Little River remember it, but I was married once for awhile. It all happened in France, and it ended in a big mess. I was almost 40 and wasn't willing to raise a child that my ex had fathered with his mistress. So he left. Thank God, we didn't have any children of our own."

We talked a long time about "hurtin' love" and stuff like that. Finally, she did say, "You know what really aggravates me?"

I said "No, what?"

Without even blinking an eye she said, "There are some days when I still miss the bastard. Even after all this time!"

I was speechless. What do you say to a comment like that? How can she miss the man after all these years? She's well into her golden years and still pining after a man who jilted her 30 or 40 years ago. This doesn't make sense. . .I thought I was supposed to have all the answers?

I did make a few of my best pontifical comments that I keep in my storehouse of pastoral wisdom. She didn't say a whole lot more about Pierre or whatever his name was.

I entertained her with a few of our sad stories and escapades about when we were all trying so hard to be Romeos. All of a sudden, she started laughing and shuffling through papers and folders in an old creaky file cabinet. She handed me a story that she swears is true. As you can tell, by now this pastoral call had turned in to a first class, story-swapping kaffeeklatsch.

I will scan the story and e-mail it over to you sometime soon. I'll warn you, everyone who reads about Ms. Demarco's valentine tears up. So tell my sweet sister-in-law to get out her hankie.

Looks like the kids were exposed to the stomach virus this a.m. at church, so I suppose we're in for it now. Any advice, Doc? I know, I know, Mom always said when the stomach virus hits, start scrubbing down the bathrooms. I remember all that, so come up with something more impressive than home remedies. Be professional, if you please. Come on! Try.

The tennis is great. These guys make it look so easy. But don't be accusing me of putting the kids in time out just so I could watch. You see, I know how your devious little mind works after all these years.....

Love and Prayers,
Wayne

Send To \ Attachments

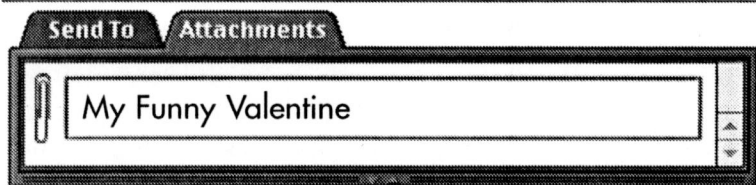

My Funny Valentine

MY FUNNY VALENTINE

For some reason, this third Valentine's Day since my divorce was bringing up a lot of sadness. A fine 'case of the blues' was blowing in, I guessed. At breakfast on this Feb. 14th, I found myself sad over the prospect of not being able to anticipate a reminder of some admirer's affections, i.e., no flowers, no candy, no candlelight. All these vacancies added up to one thing: NO ROMANCE.

Between raisin bran and sips of coffee, I talked bravely to myself about the pitfalls of having a pity party, the joys of my life as a single adult, and the bounty of God's complete love for me. I reminded myself that I had a manicure scheduled later that morning as a special treat for me on a day when treats are everywhere for everyone. After all, "Do something wonderful for yourself on February 14," had always worked as a blues chaser for me before.

Basically, my homily to myself on this Valentine's Day was, "You're fine, so don't be so whiney. Your marriage was never one built on valentines and such, so you aren't exactly used to a room full of roses." In fact, my former husband was constitutionally opposed to the sentiments expressed on February 14 because of its commercialism. He would usually grumpily comply at a minimal level, but never seemed to enjoy the love-op that the official "Love Day" afforded. My valentines to him were usually scowled upon as compliance with the materialistic dogma of our era.

After years of this dilemma, I boiled my efforts down from red satin sheets, romantic meals, candle light and such to an annual offering of a clever, whimsical but loving card...or two. When his complaints were still voiced about my surrender to Hallmarkology, I finally stood up for the red and white. One 14th of February, I declared, "It is inconceivable to me that I would NOT send my husband a Valentine." End of discussion. But nothing changed.

The post-manicure part of my sad day took me to my women's Bible Study at the church that had become my family since my divorce. This morning, the study took a sudden turn into Paul's letter to the Philippians 1:3-11. As the teacher read down through this lovely declaration of Paul's love for the Philippian church, my mind stalled out and re-wound back over 45 years to another time in my life.

I had an older connection to these verses that I had not thought about for years. It was a memory of one summer at a mountain retreat for Christians in collegiate leadership. The words of Paul suddenly became a re-tread for my worn out Valentine's Day feelings.

In a moment I recognized God's hand at work. This was my Valentine from Him! My blues vanished in a prayer of thanksgiving and praise for His lovingkindness. Just the statement, "I have you in my heart (v. 7)," was enough of a "word" from God on this day. But, the connection back to memories of that summer camp breathed a sense of romance, however wispy and imaginative, into those verses.

I began to reminisce! On the first evening of the leadership conference, my girlfriend and I were seated on the edge of the common area as people visited and made introductions. Young men shot basketballs at hoops under the lights. The cool mountain air and brilliant starlight were truly refreshing to the two of us who had just spent two days on a train. We laughed and played a game: Which guy would be your pick from this crowd of strangers?

It didn't take me long to settle on my choice. He wore a wooly, aqua sweater, and was tall, dark, and extremely handsome. In fact, he was breathtaking. "Totally out of my reach," I told my friend. Much to my surprise, as the conference went on, I found that my choice, Ron, was spending time with me and my friend. By mid-week he was frequently by my side.

We started spending most of our free time together, and one afternoon went on a long hike to enjoy the awesome scenery that surrounded the conference site. During this week I learned about the quality of this young man's life and his dedication to his future career choice in law enforcement. I liked the atmosphere of warmth and confidence that always surrounded him. His maturity and solidity were impressive, and he was determined to love and serve God.

As the conference was drawing to a close, we promised to write to one another. I agreed to this even though I knew there was little chance that a relationship would blossom since we lived on opposite sides of the USA. After the closing conference meeting, we spent a long, late evening together, and exchanged addresses. Finally the conversation had to end because I was leaving at 5 a.m. the next morning to return home. This was goodbye, and it surely had been delightful to have my "pick" pick me out of the crowd. I knew we would write.

As my friend and I prepared to leave at dawn the next morning, a very sleepy Ron came down the path to the parking lot. He was wearing his aqua sweater against the morning chill. He just wanted to say "Goodbye" again and he handed me a carefully folded note. "This is for you to read on your way back home. Just remember, I'll be praying this prayer for you." Smiling, he tapped my nose gently and we parted. The note was pressed in my hand.

It didn't take me many miles down the road to read the note from Ron. He had written down some verses from Philippians as his prayer for me as we parted:

"I thank my God every time I remember you. In all my

prayers for all of you, I always pray with joy because of your partnership in the gospel from the first day until now, being confident of this that He who began a good work in you will carry it on to completion until the day of Christ Jesus. It is right for me to feel this way about all of you, since I have you in my heart; for whether I am in chains or defending and confirming the gospel, all of you share in God's grace with me. God can testify how I long for all of you with the affection of Christ Jesus. And this is my prayer: that your love may abound more and more in knowledge and depth of insight, so that you may be able to discern what is best and may be pure and blameless until the day of Christ, filled with the fruit of righteousness that comes through Jesus Christ—to the glory and praise of God." (Phil. 1:3-11)

Ron and I corresponded for a few months, then the letters were less frequent. Finally, a note came in the mail for me in which Ron confided that he was engaged to be married. End of summer romance! All notes and letters were appropriately trashed. Tears were shed. Eventually, life absorbed this brief, sweet summer memory.

Why such a connection on this recent Valentine's Day? Certainly, God had already reminded me of His love earlier in the day over my raisin bran and coffee. I was already firmly convinced that God is the One Who is the lover of my soul. But my very own valentine from God this day was one that said, "Remember, you are someone special who can be picked out of a crowd by a wonderful man." Ron had been very complimentary of my soul, my life's vision, and the person I was on the inside and outside. In the short space of a week, our hearts had connected even though there was no future together for our lives.

All of these sentiments and memories rose to the surface as I heard these verses from Philippians read in my Bible Study on a February 14th some forty years later. And I was thankful once again for the forgotten note pressed into my hand at dawn so long ago. It was simple: as God brought the memory back, I felt special and appreciated once again. It was as if He tapped me on the nose as He dropped His valentine postmarked "From Philippi" into my heart.

Funny, isn't it?

Send To | **Attachments**

LatimerPNG@sopac.org

Subject: Moving Right Along

Now you hurt my feelings. Could you please not call any more of my stories "sappy" or "sloppy?" After all, I didn't write that one. Ms. Demarco handed it to me, and I sent it to you almost exactly like her copy. I thought it was a neat glimpse into the heart of an older single lady who has been through a lot. She has a real, honest to goodness walk with God, and obviously, He reached out to her when she was in need of some TLC. I'll bet Laurie loved it? Right?

Things have been pretty quiet lately around here. Both kids love their school, so that makes life easier on everyone. Trudy is beginning to set some things up with some of the LOV women who want to be mentored, but I'm encouraging her to not spread herself too thin.

By the by, we have talked some about a third adoption. It's about time to pursue this if we want our kids to be fairly close in age. You could pray for us about God's leading on this.

Can you imagine anyone else being Joshua and Cayla's parents? It freaks me out to think about them being in another adoptive family. We haven't mentioned this to either set of grandparents yet, so keep it quiet for now. We just need someone to help us pray for wisdom in this process. Deal?

Speaking of the adoption process, have you ever thought of all the people in the Bible who didn't finish their childhood in their birth parents' home? Look at Moses, Joseph, Samuel, David, Mephibosheth, Daniel, and Esther, just to mention the ones that come to mind right off the bat. I guess you could even say that in one way Jesus is one of those, too. His earthly father wasn't His real father. Interesting?

The Dabney's saga just goes on and on. I think their story may have the makings of my first real novel, don't you? I have another story for you about them almost finished. I'll e-mail it to you soon.

Hugs from ours to yours,
Wayne

P.S. Remind me to send Ms. Demarco a Valentine card next year. I'll have to risk making Trudy jealous!

┌───┐
│ **Send To** │ **Attachments** │
│ ┌───────────────────────────────────┐ │
│ │ Mixed Blessings   │ ▲ │
│ │   │ ▼ │
│ └───────────────────────────────────┘ │
└───┘

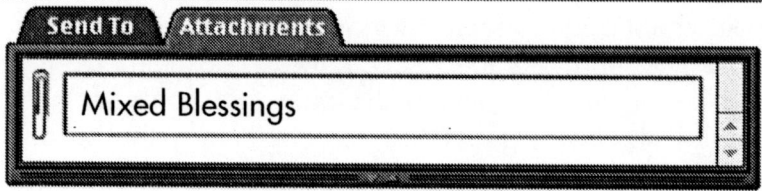

MIXED BLESSINGS

As promised, Lt. Raleigh Lawrence turned up at the Dabney residence in the late morning. He was loaded down not just with lunch, but with gifts for both Chelsea and Zachary, and a dozen red roses for Jenny. As Jenny breathed in the fragrance of her gift, she looked at Raleigh with a deadpan expression and asked, "You trying to impress us, Lieutenant?"

"How's it going?" Raleigh asked. "Am I messing up yet?"

"Nope," said Jenny, and she walked over to the dining room to get a crystal vase from Stella's china cabinet for the roses. After she arranged the flowers, she turned to Raleigh with a smile and said, "Thanks."

"Jenny, you are the queen of the one word answers."

"No way! I usually rattle on too much. Dad accuses me of having my tongue hinged in the middle."

"Well, come on then....talk to me. Like I said last night, I think we have a lot more to discuss."

Jenny was wary of pursuing anything at the moment. Since the night before, she had been trying to think clearly, but her thoughts and feelings were still reeling with this unexpected turn of events. She vacillated between being surprised and glad to see him, and wishing he'd never shown up to complicate things. She had berated herself for over twelve hours for feeding him dinner, and especially for letting him touch her, much less kiss her.

"Won't you ever learn?" She had questioned herself over

and over. Raleigh sensed her reticence, and did not press the issue. He busied himself with the children. He was thankful that Chelsea needed some help opening her gift.

Jenny finished feeding Zachary, and then they took Raleigh's carry-out meal turned 'picnic' to the shade of the big pecan tree in the back yard. This was Chelsea's favorite place for a picnic. She ran ahead of them with an old quilt, and carefully smoothed it out for everyone.

The picnic over, they gathered up the leftovers, and then stretched out on the quilt to watch the snow white clouds above them. Chelsea thought she saw a lamb, Raleigh definitely saw a space ship, and Jenny found a castle. Finally, Chelsea went off to play, and Raleigh decided to risk plunging ahead into the things he wanted to talk about.

"I almost came back last night when I thought of this, Jenny," he said as he propped himself up on one elbow.

"It's a good thing you didn't return! I crashed right after you left. Zachary never woke up, so I didn't have to feed him again. I guess all the excitement of meeting his daddy wore the little guy out. I was pretty tired too. But go on, what did you think of?"

"This is incredible. I'm not even sure I should tell you, but here goes. You remember, my father died? Well, I've always wanted to name my first born son after him," he paused while Jenny squirmed.

"Raleigh, I'm not sure we can change his name at this point," Jenny explained in her most diplomatic tone. "You see, Darcy picked it out, and we made a big deal about voting for it. We all voted 'yes' for 'Zachary.' "

Case closed.

Raleigh hesitated. "But, that's why I almost came back last night. You aren't going to believe this. There doesn't need to be any changing! My father's name was 'Zaccheus,' but everyone called him 'Zach.' "

"Oh?" said the monosyllabic queen with raised eyebrows.

Raleigh continued, "My grandma named him that because he was premature and tee-ninesy." He tried to ease the conversation away from her defensiveness. "He grew to be this huge dude, but the name never changed. Now what do you think about that?"

After a minute or two, she lowered her gaze and said quietly, "I guess I'm supposed to think that this name thing is some sort of sign. Like it's God's blessing on this little scenario? Is that what you mean?"

"Not exactly. Look, I'm glad that 'Zachary' is the name you picked." He pointed to her, then himself, "And, I'm glad that my first son has my father's name. I just wanted you to know about the coincidence. Let's let it go at that." Raleigh was as frustrated as Jenny was defensive.

"Look, Raleigh, we barely even know each other. There IS no relationship, so what do we have here?"

"I don't know, Jenny, but I'm willing to check it out. Like I told you yesterday, I decided to look you up again. Now that there is a Zachary, I'd like to see what's here for the three of us. At the very least, I'm concerned about my son. Surely, you can understand that?"

Jenny nodded, her head down.

"Jenny, I honestly don't know what the outcome of all this will be. Can you agree to this much for me?" He tried to keep a calm tone in his voice even though his feelings were way out ahead of him.

"Well, sort of. Zachary has a home, a caring family, and a church that is supportive. People are praying for us every day. I adore him. I'm not sure we need anything more at this point. I know this single parent drill, Lieutenant."

Raleigh's heart sank. He hadn't realized how much he had been counting on walking back into Jenny's life. Since he had found out about Zachary he had become even more hopeful. But, Jenny kept knocking down his dream castle.

She went on. "You know, while you were thinking all this

stuff about finding me, I've been wishing I'd never seen you. I've wanted to lose a whole chapter of my life! It's taken awhile for me to work my way back to "yes" about myself. Even now I'm not sure I'm there yet."

"I can't argue about that, Jenny. I'm really happy that you have found a way through this chaos." He paused and stretched out full length. "And your feelings about me? After all, I didn't show up for a year. I have to take the blame for that."

"Raleigh, at first I was hoping you would keep in touch. Then I found out that I was pregnant, and you don't want to know what I thought. But, I think I could've found you if I had wanted. I didn't even try because I figured your silence told me what I wanted to know. My experience with Chelsea's father left me with a lot of bad memories. I didn't want to go looking for another man who didn't care about me." She was chewing on her lower lip with a vengeance.

"So, what we are saying is that we both messed up...with more mess-up on my side than yours, in my opinion," he said as he tried to smooth out some of the struggles of the past year. "I guess you're right. We're going to have to start from zero."

Jenny nodded and leaned back against the rough bark of the tree. She stared out down the valley for a long time. Raleigh was pensive, too; but he was also enjoying watching the wind tug at Jenny's hair in the dappled sunlight. Finally, he said, as he pulled up some weeds in the lawn, "Jenny, what do you think your parents are going to think about my 're-entry' here?"

"I'm not sure, Raleigh. Right now, I'm not even sure they need to know about it." She hesitated, sighed, and then reversed her comment. "But, I guess they should know that you've been here. You are sort of a major player in this scene." She looked down at Zachary and back at Raleigh, "No one can deny that."

Raleigh reached over and touched her lower lip, and she shrank back. "Don't be so scared of me, Jenny. I promise I'm not going to hurt you. I was checking out that lip you seem so determined to chew off every time I come around."

She rubbed her lip, which had become very chapped in the last few hours. "I know, I know. My folks fuss at me all the time about that. It's a nervous habit that goes way back. At least, I've stopped carrying my security blanket."

They both laughed, and the tension was eased.

"OK, let's lighten up here," said Raleigh. "I'm looking at a lawn that needs to be mowed. Is there a mower anywhere?"

"Sure, but it's broken and stored up in that shed. See it over there in the corner by the paint cans? My Uncle Frank was supposed to come over to repair it and mow while the folks were gone. I guess he forgot that they are coming back tomorrow afternoon."

"Tomorrow!" Raleigh mouthed silently in mock terror. "Then, I'd better get busy. Mama used to have a tractor like your dad's on our place. There was no garden if I didn't keep it running. I'll go take a look at it." He walked off toward the shed, and pulled off his shirt as he went.

Jenny winced as she watched the sunlight glint off of Raleigh's muscular back. "Jeez," she breathed. She kept admiring what she saw as she kept telling herself to look the other way. She was surprised to hear him start to whistle an old hymn.

In about ten minutes, he was backing the mower out of the shed. Triumphant, he drove over to where Jenny was sitting with Zachary. He idled the motor and said, "I'm in business here. If the gas holds out, this won't take long."

Over the noise of the mower, she said, "I'll run the blower behind you. And I'll take the can over to the gas station for more gas if you need it."

Off he went. Jenny kept her eye on Chelsea and Zachary,

and moved around the yard with the blower. About half way through their chores, Pastor Wayne stopped by as Jenny had requested. The three of them sat on Vic's porch with tall glasses of iced tea. Zachary was still asleep on the quilt under the pecan tree, and Chelsea sat nearby with Raleigh's gift absorbing her attention.

By the end of the preacher's visit, there was a semblance of peace about where things stood. Raleigh felt more hopeful, and Jenny felt more comfortable with Raleigh's presence. Jenny and Raleigh decided with her Pastor's encouragement to go down to the courthouse the next morning and place Raleigh's name on Zachary's birth certificate. Raleigh was immensely relieved that something positive, however small, was happening.

As Pastor Wayne left, Jenny requested, "If you see Frank Souter, tell him not to worry about our yard." As he drove away, he was praying about the call he knew would be coming soon after the Dabneys returned from their vacation.

After the yard was finished and they had eaten a light supper, Jenny decided to go to the grocery store. She planned to have supper ready when the rest of the Dabneys returned the next evening. She asked Raleigh to move his car so she could back her car out of the garage.

"You drive a stick-shift?" Raleigh asked.

"Sure," she replied, and remembered the tears she had shed when Donny taught her to drive his old clunker of a pick up truck. He was not a patient man.

"Why don't you and Chelsea go ahead in my car. I'll stay here and tend to Zach. I think I'm too tired to move." As she reached for his keys, he pulled them away and added, "Now don't be messing with my stereo. Promise?" She agreed.

Jenny found Raleigh's car much easier to manage than Donny's old truck. As she drove off to the store, she turned up the volume on the stereo loud and clear. But she didn't change the station.

II.

The Dabneys rounded the hill toward their house.

"Looky there," said Vic. "That sorry Frank Souter kept his promise. He must've fixed my tractor."

"The yard looks great," laughed Stella. "Frank's a man of his word all right. I sure hope Zachary isn't in bed yet. Do you think Jenny will be upset that we're showing up a day early like this?"

"Oh, she will be at first. My bet is that the only thing done is this yard. We'll save her a swivette over cleaning the house and cooking up a big dinner tomorrow. She'll get over it."

Vic started to honk the horn as he drove in front of the house.

"No! Don't honk, Daddy," said Darcy. "Turn off your lights, and let's surprise her."

"OK. But she's gonna be surprised enough anyway," Vic agreed. He turned off the lights as he pulled slowly into the driveway. The three tiptoed quietly into the house. The sound of their arrival was muffled by the TV, which was blaring out the Cleveland Indians' game. Things were all tied up in the eighth inning. Raleigh was sprawled out flat on his back in front of the TV with Zachary on his bare chest. An empty bottle rolled in Raleigh's hand. Both were sound asleep.

Vic muttered, "What's going on here? Wait a minute!" his voice was getting louder. "Let me just guess." Now his voice was quite loud. He shouted, "Jennifer!"

"Shiiii—-eeoot!" Lt. Lawrence said as he stood and came to attention in one big rush. He caught himself before he saluted.

"She's not here. Sir!" said Raleigh as he held Zachary in one arm and reached for his shirt with the other.
Everyone was speechless. "Mr. and Mrs. Dabney? I'm Raleigh Lawrence."

There was a long silence. Finally, Stella asked, "Where's Jenny?"

"She's gone to the grocery store," offered Raleigh.

"Oh," was Stella's strained reply.

Darcy retrieved Zachary from Raleigh, who was still struggling with his shirt. "Are you Zachary's Daddy?" she asked.

"Well?" said Vic.

Raleigh managed to nod toward Darcy.

"Where are you staying?" growled Vic.

"Across town at Dee Wight Smith's. He's my cousin, sir."

"He was on that football team when we won district, wasn't he?" inquired Stella.

"Yes, ma'am. Now he works over at Slocum Prison as a guard."

Vic was relentless. "Did you two plan this little get together for while we were gone?"

"No, sir. I just stopped by to see Jenny. Then I found out about Zach, I mean, Zachary," he stopped, and looked down at his son in Darcy's arms.

"Well," said Vic again.

"Mr. Dabney, I think Jenny should be here before we talk about all this. Maybe I'll just wait out in front until she gets back with my car?"

"Good idea," Vic muttered as he turned to pick up the phone. "I need to call Frank and thank him for doing the yard." He pushed the speed dial button for the Souters.

Raleigh started to interrupt, then walked toward the door. Vic got Frank on the line. He turned his back and began to discuss how nice the yard looked. Then he paused, and said, "You didn't? So, how did it get mowed?"

Raleigh glanced at Stella and raised his hand.

"Hang on a sec here, Frank." The conversation paused as Stella told Vic about Raleigh's confession.

Vic explained to Frank, "Uh, Frank. Looks like Jenny

found someone to help her out since you were so late getting over here. Never could depend on you, you sorry outfit!" The phone conversation slowly wound down.

"Yeah, we came home a day early."

"Yes, I know who mowed the yard," Vic was mumbling now. "Sure, we're OK. I'll talk to you later. Maybe coffee tomorrow?" He punched off the conversation.

Vic turned around, "So, what was wrong with that mower?"

Raleigh halted in the doorway. He made his simple repairs sound serious. "I cleaned off the battery and the spark plugs, put more water in the battery, and gave it all a little extra choke. It turned over on the second try. "

"Hmph," grimaced Vic. "I guess I forgot to clean all that up last fall." The front door closed quietly as Raleigh made his exit.

Vic unloaded the luggage and camping gear from the car, and Stella began to bustle around in the kitchen. They spoke very little. She had carried in the vegetables they'd bought at the farm stand out in the country. While she was washing them off, she began cleaning up the remains of dinner still on the kitchen counter. She didn't say much until she found the leftover cornbread.

"Surely Jenny didn't use this old rusty skillet to cook cornbread in, did she?" She held up the skillet and looked up at Vic.

"She honestly made cornbread?" Jenny's incredulous father asked.

"Well, my mother would certainly like to be here to see her favorite little skillet put back into service," said Stella. "I'll just have a sample of this cornbread." And she broke off a small piece. Under her breath she muttered, "You don't suppose Raleigh made this, do you, Vic?"

"That'd be my bet," said a disgruntled Vic.

III.

The minutes dragged on and a strained balance of reticence and acceptance hovered over the Dabney home. Before too much longer, the phone rang. It was Jenny. She was in hysterics. Stella, who had answered the phone, did her best to make sense out of what she was hearing.

"Yes, honey. We're home. We're all right here. What's the matter?"

"Jenny! What's happened? Calm down so I can hear you!"

"Has there been an accident?"

"You're where?"

By now, Vic was grabbing the phone from Stella.

"Where are you, baby? Are you OK?" After a short pause, Vic added with a puzzled look, "What's that about Raleigh's car?"

"Oh," there was relief in his voice, and it was passed on to everyone in the room. "All right. We'll be right there. Just ask the store manager to call the police. And Jenny, calm down and don't let Chelsea run around. We're on our way."

Vic grabbed the keys to his pickup. "Looks like Raleigh's car has been vandalized and broken into." He rushed to the front door and called Raleigh back inside.

After Vic explained what had happened, Raleigh's first question was: "Is Jenny hurt?"

"No. But she's plenty scared. Let's get ourselves over there," urged Vic.

As soon as Vic and Raleigh reached the parking lot of the grocery store, it was easy to spot the problem. The police were there, and already had a good description of the vandals from a witness. Raleigh's collection of CDs and his new MP3 were missing. All of the windows of the Trans-Am were shattered. The once beautiful blue finish was scarred with deep gouges, and it was sprayed here and there with paint. A swastika of slimy black paint decorated the hood.

The look of terror on Jenny's face when she saw him tore at Raleigh's heart. "Jenny," he said as he put his arm around her, "these things happen." He went on, "It's just a car. It goes to the shop. It gets fixed. It's OK. It has nothing to do with you."

Slowly, Jenny's breathing returned to near-normal. "Raleigh, I was so scared when I found your car like this. Then when Mom was on the phone, I lost it." She found another tissue in her purse. "I can't believe this."

The complexities of the last twenty-four hours finally caught up with her. She wept quietly while Raleigh held her with one arm, and dug through his wallet for the identification proof that the police officer wanted. It seemed he was handling everything with one arm this evening. He had never felt so awkward.

Meanwhile, Vic put Chelsea piggyback on his shoulders while he talked to the police. They decided to have Raleigh's car towed over to the police station so it could be checked it out for evidence.

Finally, one officer took Vic aside and asked, "Mr. Dabney, is everything OK here. Could I ask you what's going on?" He nodded toward Raleigh and Jenny.

Vic looked over at Jenny in the safety of Raleigh's arm and smiled wryly. "Officer, I'm not really sure. But Jenny's hysterics seem to be the worst of it. She feels pretty bad about her friend's car."

"Oh," the officer struggled to understand. "So you are all friends?" Vic shrugged and nodded. The officer then said, "I thought maybe you were upset, or that there was something more going on here about your daughter. I hope you don't mind my asking? I'm just making sure she's all right."

"Don't worry, son. You're doing your job. I appreciate you. Jenny's over-reacted a bit. She's had a rough day or two. I think the best thing is for us all to go back home and let her calm down. Lt. Lawrence and I will worry about the car in the morning."

"Lieut…?" the policeman's voice broke off abruptly as he reassessed the situation before him and tactfully shifted the topic of conversation. "We're usually hard pressed to do much about this sort of vandalism. These wacko kids tear things up, then vanish into the pavement. But, we'll give it our best shot and see if we can bring them in. " He and Vic shook hands. He had another brief conversation with Raleigh before they all left.

As the four walked to Vic's pickup, Jenny said with her typically wry sense of humor, "Welcome home, Daddy-O!" Vic handed Chelsea his keys so she could run ahead and punch the button that would unlock his truck. Raleigh's arm never left Jenny's shoulders.

Send To **Attachments**

LatimerPNG@sopac.org

Subject: Hang In There

Hi, Chuck and Laurie:

Thanks for that recent long e-mail. Sorry to hear that things have been tough lately. I guess the Gospel doesn't sound like Good News to your new friends right now. We will increase the prayers going up from the LOV community here.

I know you'll remember EmmaLu Sparks, Ed's wife? She was the one everyone was so convinced was my "match made in heaven?" Everyone was convinced but yours truly, that is! Because we've been friends for so long, the Sparks have been a great couple for us to lean on and hang out with. They are always willing to pitch in whenever I need something extra done. Their kids and ours play endlessly together.

Ed and I have great laughs remembering high school football stories. I try not to remember that I was just the water boy on that famous team we were all on. Funny, all the bad plays we grieved over way back when are today's great party stories.

The Sparks' gift of helping showed up in an unbelievable way recently. The story that follows is one that must be told. I hope my literary talents can do it justice.

I asked EmmaLu to run an errand for me when we were both totally stressed out after a Building and Grounds Committee meeting. (Have I told you how much I dislike/hate/abhor committee meetings? I do.) This story is what EmmaLu shared with us when she came by the day after the errand.

I asked her to take something to the prison, and what was supposed to be a drop off at the prison gate, turned into a nightmare or a divine appointment, depending on your point of view. She was so excited about how God used her even when she was tired, worried about Ed and the kids, pissed at me, hungry, and definitely not pre-pared for what happened. You'll like this one.

Hang in there with the Gospel. Nobody said this would be easy. Make Jesus and Paul proud. And don't forget to do a bit of medicine in your spare time. That'll make Luke proud! Me? I'm always proud!

Greetings to everyone out yonder,
Wayne

```
Send To    Attachments
┌─────────────────────────────────┐
│ Divine Appointment              │
│                                 │
└─────────────────────────────────┘
```

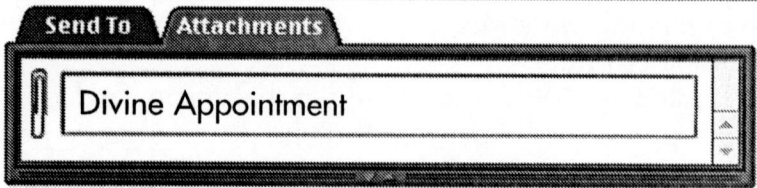

DIVINE APPOINTMENT

The committee meeting of the Lily of the Valley Community Church was winding down. There was the usual clutter of used styrofoam cups, wadded up paper napkins, and crumbs from the cookies brought by the "R's," the alphabetical appointees for bringing refreshments. The meeting had been about the new church parking lot. The sea of mud that everyone had to deal with on rainy Sundays definitely needed to be paved. The discussion had stalled out over how many visitors' parking places to reserve, and whether the stripes should head straight in or be angled. Time had run out, and everyone had to leave to do afternoon errands. Very little had been resolved.

As EmmaLu Sparks turned to leave, the preacher walked up and took her elbow to speak with her. She wondered in a flash what she could do about the lines on the parking lot. Surely Wayne didn't think that she could mediate between Pearle and Jo Lena. They'd been scrapping like wet cats since they were cheerleaders together in high school. She knew she didn't want to get in between the two of them at this point.

But, that wasn't it at all. He wanted her to do him a favor.

"All right, I guess I will if I can, Wayne," she heard herself reply. "Depends on what it is?" She was running down her mental list of friends who could pick up the carpool for her if this was going to be a long errand.

The preacher turned his back to Sally Mix, another committee member, and quietly explained his request.

"EmmaLu, could you take some clothes over to Slocum Prison for Perry Mix? I'd be much obliged if you could help me out with this."

EmmaLu felt herself shift into reverse. This would take forever, and would get her home well after dark. After all, there were other people who lived out that way. There was no way she should even think about doing this.

"I....don't. But....isn't? I mean, didn't we just pray for him and all that about, you know....that deal tonight?" She was talking with her eyes squeezed shut.

"Shhhhh! Pipe down! I don't want Sally to hear us talking about this. But that's what the clothes are for, EmmaLu. They are for afterwards. The warden called me because they couldn't find Perry's parents. For some reason, we're still listed on Perry's documents as his church. I have been out there and seen him a few times. I guess they don't know about his sister, Sally. The rest of his family has apparently skipped out to Florida for the big event. Sally is just barely hanging on. I think she was crying during most of the meeting today. I'm not even sure if she is going over to Slocum tonight. The execution is at 7."

Wayne continued, "I can't go out there because of the church session meeting here at 6:30. I can't miss it; there are some big decisions pending. I was able to get some clothes together from the Serve the Sheaves Closet. Look, what do you think about these?" He held open a crumpled WalMart bag, also donated to the Serve the Sheaves Closet. Inside the bag was an oddly matched set of nondescript cords and a blue button-down shirt. There was also a red, white, and black striped tie with ducks embroidered on the black part.

"They're just fine, Wayne," EmmaLu whispered. "But are you sure I'm the one to do this." She knew she was beginning to beg off. She also knew it wasn't working.

"EmmaLu, please. I've already asked around," he pleaded.

EmmaLu and Wayne had known each other forever. Their parents had been close friends before either of them was born. Everyone had thought that they would eventually marry, but it just never happened. However, they had a unique closeness that was born out of those early connections.

"Wayne, you can't be serious," she hissed, knowing all the time he was, and that she couldn't turn him down. "Will they let me in? I had clearance one time for the women's ministry stuff we used to do over there, but I doubt I'm still on the list at the gate."

"I'll call up to the gate and see what I can do about clearance for you. Trust me, they'll let you in. They don't want any more bad press at Slocum about this execution," he continued. "Please just help me out, and thanks a bunch if you can. I'll really owe you one. Look, I'll call Trudy and have her swing by for your carpool."

Trudy was the girl Wayne married when everyone said that she was not good enough for him. Turns out she was almost an angel. EmmaLu knew that Wayne could be stubborn as a mule with a sore hoof. Right now was a good example. She might as well cooperate.

"Oh, OK," snapped EmmaLu as she grabbed the bag from the reverend, and ran for the phone to call Ed.

"Lu, can't you ever just say 'No?'" growled Ed.

"You don't know how many times I tried to say 'No,' but it looks like Wayne really is in a bind."

"Oh, go on. Just give us a call when you leave Slocum if you can." EmmaLu knew exactly how his eyebrows were drawn together now. Well, she didn't like this any more than he did, and he was staying home. She told him to look for some change in the blue cup on the kitchen windowsill, and to take the kids out to dinner. She also suggested that he could calm down a bit and quit frowning.

EmmaLu grabbed a handful of the "R's" cookies as she

ran out of the portable building where the committee had met. As she drove away, EmmaLu saw Sally Mix swing into traffic behind her in the distance. Poor Sally. Must be tough having a criminal for a brother. No one talked to her after the meeting. But she never talked either. In fact, she had been silent through most of their meetings. So what could she expect?

EmmaLu's mind buzzed with the favor she was performing. First of all, why did it have to be her? Why did everyone always ask her to do the yucky things? Why couldn't one of the men go over there? Why didn't Wayne, THE pastor, think he needed to be there tonight?

"What's the deal with our church?" Her feelings roiled. "We can't even get a parking lot paved. Now Sally is all by herself for her brother's execution. And I'm holding a bag of used clothes for his funeral." She was getting more furious all the time.

Her mind raced on. "Why didn't the Mixes take some clothes over to Slocum for Perry? I'll bet they won't even be back here in time for his funeral." She hit the steering wheel and grimaced when she thought about the rest of the Mix family watching the sunset in Florida while she delivered the clothes for this really scuzzy guy who had molested and murdered three little kids from down river. No doubt that he did it. Perry Mix had definitely been no count since she had first known him in the third grade.

The Mixes had visited the Lily of the Valley Community Church off and on for years. The parents stopped coming to church years ago, and Perry never came much even when he was a child. When Sally Mix came back to town after having a baby out of wedlock, she started coming every Sunday to church. She even rededicated her life one night on a church bus trip to a Billy Graham Crusade. To her credit, she had gone to work at the local grocery store. Ever since then she had held tenaciously to her job and her room at

Mountain Views Boarding House.

The guard at the Slocum Prison gate turned the green light on as EmmaLu approached. Wayne must've gotten through to the gatehouse because the guard waved her on through without checking anything. There was a crowd of TV cameras and reporters clustered by the gate, but EmmaLu breezed past them and went on inside the walls of the prison. She was puzzled by the commotion around the gate until she remembered the media was covering the different groups for and against capital punishment.

As she ran into the main entrance, she saw Sally coming through the gates in the distance. Probably by now Sally had seen her and was wondering why she was here. She'd have to explain later. Now if she could get the clothes to the right place, she could turn the car around and head for home and her family. She didn't like it when Ed was grumpy, and she knew he was. She liked it even less when she was grumpy at the same time, and she had to admit that she was. The guard at the entry desk looked up, and EmmaLu gave him a brief explanation.

"Mizriz Sparks, let me check downstairs." He buzzed himself through the door and was gone. Pretty soon, Sally came through the entrance looking like she was going to be sick.

"Hi, Sally," smiled EmmaLu.

"Hey, there," replied a puzzled Sally. "Are you here for . . . .?" She left her question in mid-air.

"No," EmmaLu rushed in. "Well, sort of. You see, Brother Wayne asked me to run out here for him. I have some clothes for after…. I'm sorry, Sally. I don't know what to say. The clothes are for Perry when it's over." Now EmmaLu felt sick.

"Oh," sighed Sally. EmmaLu could tell she had been crying. "I guess I never even thought of that. I wonder why they called the church?"

"Well, it doesn't matter now. It's all taken care of. Are you going to be OK?" EmmaLu asked.

"I guess so. I'd like for all this to just go away, especially tonight. Bubba's been in trouble for so long. It's like a bad dream I can't wake up from. I always hoped he would get himself straightened out."

The guard came back through the door and looked through the odd assortment of clothing that EmmaLu had handed him. Then he nodded toward Sally. "You can go down and talk to him now. I need your signatures, and I need to see a photo ID of some sort. Let's see, ma'am, you're family?" Sally nodded. EmmaLu blinked and gulped, but the guard never looked her way.

"You can have 15 minutes to visit with Mr. Mix, and then the warden and other officers will take over. Mr. Mix can only have two visitors, so I guess you two are it." He handed Sally his pen, and waited for her to find her driver's license.

EmmaLu's mind was whirling. What could she say to say, 'NO!'? Ed was right. She was going to have to learn to say it and mean it. Instead, she gasped for air and reached out to Sally.

"Is anyone in your family coming to be with you, Sally?"

All Sally could do was shake her head. She was now embarrassed as well as scared and sad.

"Do you want me to stay with you? I won't run off if you want me to stay." EmmaLu saw the desperation in Sally's eyes and knew. There was no way she could leave now. She signed the list on the guard's clipboard, and showed him her license. He handed her back the sack full of Perry's clothes.

The door was buzzed open for them, and EmmaLu was in the chute with Sally who was going to death row to say goodbye to her brother before he was executed. She felt like she was caught in an undertow. It was like when she was a little girl at the beach and felt the strong current pulling all around her.

"I cannot believe this! What am I going to say? How do I get into these things?" Her thoughts kept careening around in her mind as they boarded the elevator bound for death row.

Sally was clinging to her now, and she'd better be ready to be the strong one. Was "strong" the right term? EmmaLu really wasn't sure. The elevator bumped, everyone stumbled, and they went on down. Sally had already squeezed her hand until it ached.

EmmaLu had a thought that lasted only a millisecond. It was like Jesus said to her, "EmmaLu, calm down. I know about these things." She responded to Him just as briefly with a mental sniff, "I guess you do know about executions." The elevator sighed to a stop, and they were all walking down the hall at a rapid pace.

Beyond the counter at the end of the hall sat Dee Wight Smith. The huge black prison guard stood up and greeted the three. "Good! Glad you folks are here. Perry and me was wondering who'd come."

EmmaLu had graduated from high school with Dee Wight. They had become friends because his name was next to Ed's on the class seating charts and the guys had been teammates in football.

"Thanks for being here, EmmaLu," he said quietly to her as they were ushered down the hall by the other guard. She tried to smile, but her mouth wouldn't cooperate. Dee Wight opened a door by punching in a code.

There was Perry Mix seated at a table with a dinner tray in front of him. He gulped down his last bite of food when they entered the room. No one spoke in the brief, tense silence. It was Perry who spoke first, "Well, why don't everyone set theirselves down?" Metal chairs were scraped over to the table.

Dee Wight tried to put everyone at ease, "I been knowing all you people for a long time, and I know this ain't an easy thing for a family or for friends. Me and Perry been doing a lots of talking here the last few weeks, and I think he's OK. He knows what he done, and that it has all finally come down to tonight." His eyes were focused on Perry, and Perry gave a brief nod.

Dee Wight went on. "Me and him just been hanging out down here together trying to pass the time. I been reading some to him from the Bible your preacher left with him. But he don't want a chaplain here or anyone like that. He also has requested that we keep everything as simple as possible."

Sally reached over and patted Perry's hand with hers. He began to cry. "I'm sorry, Bubba. I wish this could've turned out different. I guess I don't know what else to say." Tears engulfed both of them, and Sally gave him a stiff hug. EmmaLu still hadn't said a word.

Dee Wight looked up at EmmaLu, and made one of those requests. "EmmaLu, I wonder if you could say a prayer for us before the warden comes in?"

How could she say "No?" The other guard shifted nervously and looked out of the small window in the door.

EmmaLu couldn't think how to start. Her mouth was powdery dry. In another one of those milliseconds that she and Jesus seemed to be sharing this evening, she hurled a silent prayer at the ceiling, "Jesus! What would You pray?"

She plunged back into reality with a very small voice, and prayed. "Jesus, thank You for being here with us, and for walking beside us in good times and bad. We especially ask You to be with Perry right now. Give him a calm heart as You reach out for him. Thank You that You know all about executions... You had one, too. Thank You for Your cross. We all stand together in its shadow tonight." There was a short, heavy silence. Dee Wight said in a tearful voice, "Thank You, Lord Jesus. Amen and Amen." Everyone was sniffling.

EmmaLu blew her nose on a used-by-the-kids tissue she

dug out of her jacket pocket, and said, "Sally, I'll be outside the door. You and Perry can visit until the warden comes in."

She gave Perry a quick glance, but he still had his head bowed. She left the room, and was flooded with relief when the door closed softly behind her. She waited. In a moment, the guard from upstairs opened the door and left. He returned shortly with the warden and several other officials. When they pushed the door code and walked in, Dee Wight came out bawling like a baby.

After a moment to compose himself, he said, " 'Law, EmmaLu, you pray powerful. The Lord's strong in you tonight." He grinned at her with the brilliant smile that had always been his, and she knew she was all right. It was like at the beach when her dad would rush into the surf and grab her up and out of the undertow. Now she simply wanted to go home and tell Ed how Wayne's little request had taken on a life of its own.

"Come on down here to my station, and let's get us a cold drink," Dee Wight said as they walked back down to his desk. "I wasn't so sure how you was handling things back there when you walked out."

"I guess I'm OK, Dee Wight. I'm not even supposed to be down here. That guard thought I was family with Sally and gave me clearance at the same time with her."

"C'mon! You're joking now?" Dee Wight looked shocked. "I thought you were someone official from that church you and the Mixes belong to."

She shook her head. "I was dropping off some clothes for Perry and found out Sally was over here by herself." She handed him the WalMart sack that had been her invitation to this bizarre experience. "This is something for Perry to wear for the funeral." He put the clothes in a box marked 'Perry Mix.' She took a long swallow from the can Dee Wight had brought her out of his little refrigerator.

Dee Wight left her with her own thoughts for a moment,

then changed the subject. "Sometimes, EmmaLu, the nights are really long down here, and you know what I do?"

When she shook her head, he kept on talking and smiling. "I dream about catching those long, beautiful passes your Ed used to throw me the year we won district. My, my, how we loved to play football. Remember?"

"Remember? Of course I do. I was right there, too. I always thought you and Ed would be playing in the Super Bowl someday." They kept reminiscing as the moments played out toward 7 o'clock. The black man kept his eye on the clock. Just before the appointed time, he held up his hand and bowed his head until the moments had passed along with Perry Mix.

Eventually, the officials filed out, shook hands all around, offered canned remarks, and boarded the elevator with the upstairs guard. Sally stood quietly in their wake at Dee Wight's counter. He brought her a cold drink. They all wiped their eyes and felt self-conscious. EmmaLu shared the remains of the "R's" cookies.

Finally, Sally said in a tear soaked voice, "EmmaLu, your prayer really sank in with Bubba."

"Really? I can't even remember what I said, Sally. I just know it was short," blinked EmmaLu.

"That part about Jesus understanding executions."

"Oh, that?" EmmaLu replied in a stunned voice. "I never thought of that myself until we were coming down on the elevator. I guess you could say that Jesus gave me that. No, I know He did. It was like He spoke to me in my head. I was really scared, and that thought definitely calmed me down."

"Well, it worked for Perry, too. He said it helped him get a grip. Then, you want to know what he said?" They waited for her to bring her tears under control again. "He said, 'Me and Jesus can swap stories. I'll ask Him more about it all in about 15 minutes.'"

"Then the warden interrupted us and Bubba never

balked. He stood up, gave me the peace sign, and said, 'I'm ready.' Those men were really floored. I know Perry can be pretty hard to manage sometimes, and they were prepared for him to go ballistic on them."

"Well, I'll swan. Now that's beautiful," said Dee Wight in a rough whisper.

Sally shrugged. "What do I do now, Dee Wight?" she asked.

"Sign these papers the warden left here for you, and give them to the guard upstairs. From then on, it's all been arranged by the funeral home. You go on home and rest up. After the funeral, maybe you should get away…like go to Florida or something," answered Dee Wight.

"I don't think Florida is the place for me right now," she answered with a grimace.

EmmaLu wanted to have a finger-pointing lecture with all of Perry Mix's family down in Florida right now. How could they leave poor Sally to go through this alone?

In a moment, Sally asked, "Dee Wight, did Bubba tell you that whatever is left in his bank account is for you?" Dee Wight nodded as tears slid down his face. He stood up and punched his big fist into the cinder block wall. Pretty soon they walked together to the elevator. Dee Wight told EmmaLu to say "hello" to Ed.

"Tell him if he ever wants to throw a football around to look me up. And be sure the guard upstairs helps you ladies through all that ruckus up there by the front gate."

Upstairs, EmmaLu called home and left Ed a message on their answer machine that she was leaving. The two women followed each other through traffic and back to Little River. EmmaLu waved Sally over just before she turned up the hill to the Mountain Views Boarding House.

"I'll call you before the funeral. If you want, Ed and I will come by and pick you up. Do you think you'll be OK tonight," she shouted over the traffic from her car window.

Sally nodded an affirmative reply. "I just need a bowl of cereal and a good night's sleep. Bubba and I are both at peace now. I'm sad, but I'm OK, thanks to the word that Jesus gave you. And thanks for staying with me, EmmaLu. It really helped me get through this." Because it was starting to rain, neither woman lingered.

When EmmaLu pulled the car into the garage and went in the house, she realized that the house was shut down for the night. Ed and the kids were already in bed. He woke up enough to hear a brief description of her errand, and she heard an even shorter account of what he and the kids had done. EmmaLu asked him if he could get off work so they could take Sally to Perry's funeral, and he agreed to try. They were both too tired to talk very long.

As EmmaLu drifted off to sleep, she jolted awake. "Great! We forgot about planning for handicapped parking in that new parking lot. Pearle will totally freak out if she has to re-draw everything. I'll be painting the stupid lines on by myself at this rate," she muttered.

"For Pete's sake, what's up now, Lu?" Ed sputtered up out of a sleepy fog.

"Never mind," she whispered. She patted his strong arm as he drew her closer to him. They were asleep in no time.

Send To | **Attachments**

LatimerPNG@sopac.org

Subject: Better Than Fiction

I've been laughing all day! I finished helping Trudy put the kids to bed and decided I couldn't resist sending an e-mail over to you about this one. I ran into Dee Wight Smith this morning, and he had me in stitches. I guess he'll never let his cousin forget about this chapter out of their lives. Anyway, I thought you two would get a kick out of this story. It really is almost word for word like Dee Wight told me.

By the way, Rosetta Lawrence, Raleigh's mother, is still here and has made quite an impression on all of us. I have my own suspicions as to why she has stayed so long. Everyone thinks that she is here to sweep up after Raleigh and see her grandson, but personally I think she has her eye on the preacher out at Galilee Valley Church. He's been a life long bachelor, but we'll see!

Bye now,
Wayne

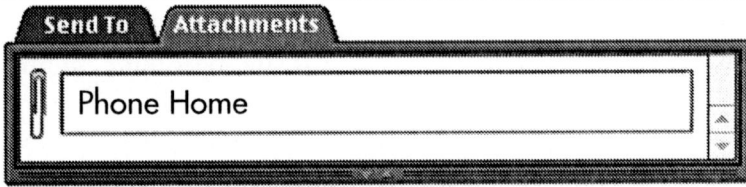

PHONE HOME

"Yes, Mama," Raleigh mumbled into the telephone. "Yes, you heard me right." On purpose, he had made this call very early in the morning to catch his mother in her best mood. Early morning was when she read her Bible and talked out loud, very loud, to God.

"Yes, Ma'am. I know, I know!" he said and drummed his pen on the arm of the chair. He was in the living room of Dee Wight's small apartment. He looked over sheepishly at his cousin who was there with him for moral support. Dee Wight did not need to listen on the other phone to fill in the rest of the one-sided conversation he was hearing.

"But, I just found out myself a few days ago, Mama."

"She's a girl I had a blind date with last year when I was visiting Dee Wight on furlough."

"That's right. Only one date."

"No, no plans for that. We're going to talk about it."

"Now, Mama, please don't go there. I'm not usually that sort. You know me better than that."

"I don't know. Mama, it just happened."

"Of course I remember what you told me about protection."

"It's 'Jennifer,' and just for the record, she's,. . ." he hesitated, "she's pretty special." Dee Wight was beginning to enjoy this.

"She named him 'Zach.'"

"Now how could she possibly know Poppa's name was 'Zaccheus?' Anyway, the little guy's name is 'Zachary'."

"Well, count it up, Mama." Raleigh was miserable and trying hard not to be too sarcastic. "Right, he's three months old."

"He looks fine to me. He favors our family, mostly me."

"Mmm-hmm. I've seen him a lot. I've even changed some diapers."

"Yes, Ma'am, I've met them. They're nice folks. Good people. They go to church and have a nice place. He's a builder and her mother runs a beauty shop. Jenny directs a day care center over at their church."

"It's hard to say. As far as I can tell, they seem to be doing OK with all this. They have really supported Jennifer with Zach. She has another child, a cute little girl named 'Chelsea.' Jennifer has a younger sister, I think her name is 'Darcy,' and they all live together.

"Well, they believe in taking care of their family, Mama. You ought to know how that feels."

"It's Dabney."

"I don't know. What do you expect? I think they like me OK, but no one sees this as a great thing, you know. I haven't been real high on their list for obvious reasons. The best thing about it all is Zachary. We'll just have to see what happens from here on."

"You're what?" he asked incredulously and rolled his eyes.

"Now, hold on, Mama. You don't have to come up here. Please, just stay there. Let me take care of this. This is my problem to work out. Zachary is my son, you know"

"Yes, I'm sure he's mine." There was a long pause while Raleigh listened with the phone held about an inch away from his ear.

"OK, OK! You're determined," he conceded with a growl. "When? I only have a few days left on my leave. I don't know about this, Mama." He was not happy.

"Today? That soon?" He glared at his cousin. "The last bus? I guess I'll be there. "

Raleigh started to hang up when he saw Dee Wight gesturing frantically about something. He gave him a quick nod of agreement.

"Mama, wait. Don't hang up yet. Since you're coming, you should probably know something before you arrive. Zachary's mother is a white girl."

"You there?"

"Hold on! Chill, Mama. I don't think color is a huge deal right now. We all just met, and we're trying to get acquainted. OK?"

"Please, don't worry so much. Calm down. I'm going to be fine and so is my baby boy. You don't have to be in charge of this, Mama."

"Yeah. I won't be late. I'll be there."

"I love you, too."

The phone was dropped sloppily back onto its cradle. Raleigh groaned and slouched further down in the chair. He covered his face with his hands. As he looked between his fingers at Dee Wight, he could tell that his cousin had been having far too much fun with this conversation.

"This is funny?" he moaned.

"Well…..?" Dee Wight grinned.

"Can you believe Rosetta is hauling herself up here today?"

"Are you really surprised, Ral?"

"I guess not. Rosetta can sure complicate things."

"You knew before you called that she would want to get her hands on that baby didn't you? He's her first grandson!"

"Sure, but, TODAY?" The moaning and grimacing continued. "I guess I'd better call and tell Jenny about all this."

Dee Wight pulled his large frame up out of his recliner. If there was one thing he'd learned as a prison guard, it was how and when to distract men from dwelling on their problems.

"Tell you what. You can call Jenny later when you've had a chance to think on this awhile. Let's drive out to the farm and see if Aunt Rosetta can stay with my folks while she's here." He knew full well that she would be more than welcome. "I need to help Dad this morning with a heavy chore or two out there, and you can lend me a hand."

"Great idea, Dee. I hadn't even thought yet about where she would stay." Raleigh grabbed his keys and was already out the door. "Some diversion sounds good," he muttered over his shoulder. "Just don't let me forget to meet that last bus."

"How about some hoops when we get back? I could use some exercise. We should be back to town before noon," asked Dee Wight. This was another question he knew the answer to before he asked. These two had pursued a basket-ball grudge match since childhood.

"Fine, fine. You're on. How much you putting up for the first game?" Dee Wight held up two fingers.

"You're so cheap! You'd better mean dollars?"

The cousins walked to the car. Raleigh slowed down enough to take a long look at the fresh paint on his Trans-Am. As he started around to the driver's side, he reached over and swatted Dee Wight on the back of the head.

"Thanks for the use of your phone, Uncle Dee."

"Any time you need back-up when you phone home, I'm here for you, big guy." Fortunately, he was quick enough to dodge a more serious swing from his Cousin Raleigh.

LatimerPNG@sopac.org

Subject: New Clinic Congrats!

Hi. How are my favorite Martians, I mean missionaries? Honest, I really do feel like you are living on another planet. I hope you are taking lots of videos and pictures so we can have a visual on how life goes on your planet.

I'm glad you enjoyed Raleigh's call to his mother. They really are quite a pair. They love each other, but pretty much stay on each other's case all the time. It'll be interesting to see how all this works out.

Right now, it's about 50/50 whether Jenny and Raleigh will make it. They are devoted to parenting Zachary, but have very little to base a relationship on at this early date. You never know? God is definitely growing them up. Whether or not they grow together remains to be seen.

I don't know if you will call this next story "entertaining" or not. It is about the kind of people who can really make a difference in someone's life. I wish we had more folks like the Blackwells. They are working the farm at the old home place that Will inherited. They have restored it and cleaned it all up. Now they are trying to turn themselves into farmers.

I went out and rode shotgun on the tractor with Will the other day. Really a beautiful experience. I can see why farmers like what they do. To be outside like that day after day could become addictive. We really couldn't talk much over the sound of the tractor, but I thoroughly enjoyed just being out there with Will.

It was great to hear about the opening of your new clinic, Dr. Chuck. Congratulations! Send pictures ASAP. Is there anything you need for your new digs that we could send from here? More of those rainbow bandaids? You know we're always looking for projects and fundraisers. Plus, I do want you to have what you need to do Our Father's business. Let us know. I'm serious.

Love you guys,
Wayne

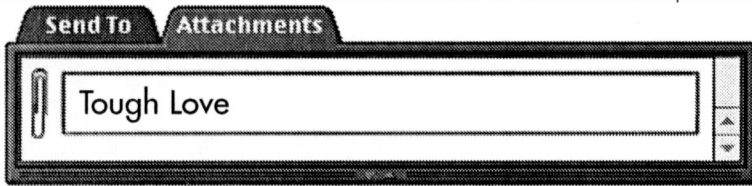

```
┌─────────────────────────────────────┐
│ Send To  Attachments                │
│  ┌───────────────────────────────┐  │
│  │ Tough Love                    │  │
│  └───────────────────────────────┘  │
└─────────────────────────────────────┘
```

TOUGH LOVE

Caroline Blackwell looked with wonder at the infant beside her. So small and sweet. A brand new life, and her name was 'Andrella.' As they drove away from Riverton General Hospital, the warm sunshine fell across the baby's face. The two newly matched residents of Little River made their way up the valley to the Blackwells' farm.

Caroline's happiness with her role in Andrella's life was also part of the warmth in the car that morning. What a thrill to leave the hospital with a newborn when you are already through having babies of your own. She was overwhelmed with the privilege that was hers as a foster parent. This was not her first experience at fostering. She and her husband, Will, had taken several children into their licensed foster home. But the newborns held a particular fascination for Caroline.

The Blackwells kept an array of supplies on hand to suit the needs of children that came into their home. Each child also had a small allowance from the county that could be spent on specific needs. So after a quick call to Will who was out on the tractor tilling their land for the next crop, she had been very busy. Will said he would try to shut things down and come in earlier than usual this afternoon. Thankfully he had been able to hear his cell phone ringing over the noise of the tractor.

After the call from the Human Services social worker, Caroline had run all over the community borrowing back nursery equipment that was loaned out to other foster parents. The foster parent organization kept an active inventory of large and expensive items that were necessary for the different stages of parenting. In the short space of an hour or two, she was able to gather together a bed and changing table. She kept an umbrella stroller at home because children always need a stroller.

Caroline went next to one of the local discount stores where she bought new baby clothes and odds and ends such as diapers and baby shampoo. Thankfully, the hospital had sent them home with quite a supply of formula as well as a teddy bear, and a receiving blanket made by the hospital volunteers.

As the farm grew closer, Caroline thought about the whole process of being a foster parent. It was not as easy or as difficult as people thought. The hard part was the preparation and the mental stamina a family had to bring to the fostering arena. The easy part for Caroline was the role as a parent. Often people would say to her, "Oh, I could never do that. I would get too attached."

But Caroline and Will were actually well trained professional public servants. They knew the boundaries that are involved in fostering. When the time came for the child to move to another setting, their attitudes were in place to facilitate that step. It was difficult, but God had always helped them deal with the grief of seeing one of their "kids" move on. The blessings of loving the child while he or she was with them far out-weighed the losses.

The county caseworker had assured Caroline that all their paper work and their license was current and up to date. Their home had recently been inspected, and their medical exams were current. She and Will had just completed the necessary on-going training to keep their license valid.

Another thing Caroline had done before going to the hospital to pick up Andrella was to review her materials on respiratory monitors and CPR for infants. Andrella would be wearing a monitor for at least three months. With a sigh of relief, she decided that they were as ready as they could be for this new arrival into their home.

As she drove home, she was rehearsing in her mind how to tell the other foster children in their home why this baby needed a monitor and why she might cry more than other babies they'd had in the past. Carrie, 6, and Troy, 10, were old enough to understand that sometimes babies born to parents with problems like drug addiction arrive on this planet with their parents' addictions.

Andrella was one of those infants. During Andrella's delivery, it was discovered that her mother, Tina, was addicted to cocaine. Because she also had the mother's cocaine in her blood stream, the little girl would have to be carefully monitored for complications that might develop. The doctors felt like this baby had a good chance of overcoming her problems, but her need for a monitor indicated that she was not totally out of the woods.

Caroline and Andrella arrived home as the county caseworker pulled into the driveway. After the usual excitement of settling the baby into her newly arranged nursery, the caseworker sat down with Caroline. They went over the baby's needs and her family circumstances. Will made it home in time for most of their discussion.

Caroline asked if they could call their new foster child 'Andy' because 'Andrella' seemed like such a mouthful. But the caseworker reminded her that it was important to keep the baby's family of origin system intact. That meant using her unusual name. The caseworker explained that she had been named for her father, Andre, who was now serving time at Slocum Prison for trafficking in drugs. Andrella's maternal grandmother was named 'Ella.' So now the name at least made sense even if it was hard to get used to saying it.

Tina was going into a drug rehabilitation program, an option offered her after her addiction was discovered. At first, the hospital staff was not at all sure that Tina was interested in this option. In fact, she had left the hospital and abandoned her daughter before either was dismissed. Everyone at the hospital nursery was delighted when Tina called in twelve hours later, and said she was willing to go into rehab if she could eventually have her daughter back. The social workers assured her that she could indeed parent her daughter if over time she proved to be a trustworthy, drug-free mother. Consequently, as soon as Tina made her plans known, Andrella was put into foster care until her mother finished the rehab program.

Caroline knew from her training that the major focus of the foster care system was to re-unite the birth family. Happy endings often started out with just this sort of commitment by one parent. Sadly, though, these happy endings were few and far between. In Andrella's case, her mother's sudden commitment to seek help was driven by a two-fold purpose. Not only did Tina want to keep her baby, but she also saw a chance to break away from her desperate surroundings. Everyone she knew was an addict, so where else could she turn?

It had taken Tina only twelve hours back in her old neighborhood to decide that she did not want to continue living at this level. As soon as she put her decision in motion, she was amazed at the concern and care that was out there for her. The good people who came out of nowhere to help seemed like her own private miracle. Now she had a chance to break her addictions to cocaine and bad relationships. And she had hope for a decent life for herself and her daughter. The caseworkers located a church, The Galilee Community Church, that was willing to sponsor Tina in her efforts. The congregation was willing to become her new family and friends. Tina saw this offer of rehabilitation as her golden ring, and she grabbed it.

The caseworker told every detail of Andrella's short life

and troubled family to the Blackwells. In return, they asked every question they could think of. They wanted to provide an atmosphere that would enhance every strong point possible for this little girl. Understanding the birth family was a big part of good fostering. Then the caseworker shifted the conversation to Caroline and Will.

"I know you have agreed to take Andrella into your home, but I need to know how you are doing personally with this placement. Are you ready for another infant in your home yet?" There was a long silence while the Blackwell's processed the question and struggled to answer honestly.

They had lost a foster baby to Sudden Infant Death Syndrome about 9 months before. It was one of the worst experiences either of them had ever been through, and it had lingering effects on both of them. The baby had taken her usual nap in the afternoon. When Caroline went in to check on her after the normal naptime had come and gone, she found the little girl was not breathing. She immediately began CPR on her in her arms as she ran out the back door to call Will who was in the barn repairing some of his equipment. Together they rushed her to Riverton General Hospital, but when they arrived, it was too late to revive her.

The Blackwells grieved for weeks afterwards, and the caseworker knew that they still struggled with the feelings of guilt and sadness at times. The little girl had only been with them for a few months, but they were not the kind of foster parents who waited very long to fall in love with their foster children.

Finally, Will spoke up, "I know we will never forget what happened to that little angel on our watch, but I think we've finally managed to resolve our issues about it. I think the worst thing would be for us to withold care from a baby who needs us because we are still grieving. Losing one precious little one shouldn't keep us from taking care of others. That would compound the loss, in my opinion."

Caroline agreed with Will. The caseworker was satisfied that Andrella would have the full attention of the Blackwells and would most likely thrive in their care.

Caroline went on to say, "You know, I don't think I had thought of this before, but losing Heather, the teenage girl we planned to adopt, was equally as tragic a loss to our whole family. The double loss of the two of them nearly did me in as far as fostering goes."

The caseworker looked up from the paperwork that she was completing for Andrella's placement and said, "I didn't know about a Heather? That must've happened before I was hired by the county."

"Well, she lived with us for three years and was in and out of trouble the whole time. We had planned to adopt her, but we just never could come up with a family plan that worked for her. She was very oppositional in the way she did life, and the county finally removed her and put her in residential treatment. It just never would come together for us with Heather after that."

Will chimed in, "I don't think I have ever seen Caroline so consistently upset over such a long period of time than when we were going through all that. Everything we tried was sabotaged by Heather, and all the while we were both crazy about her. She looked enough like our brood to be ours, and at times would fit in so well. We would get things all smoothed out, and she'd stir things up again." He shook his head as he remembered how tough those days were.

Then he went on, "My struggle in resolving our situation with Heather was mostly about me. I would get so frustrated with her, and I lost my temper with her on a regular basis. I've always felt like maybe I was responsible somehow for the whole thing falling through."

The caseworker had been flipping back in the Blackwell's file as they talked about Heather. "I see here that you both went through some counseling after she was removed from you home. And down here on this page it says that you are no longer interested in an adoption."

"That's correct," agreed Caroline. "The other thing that we rewrote in our contract was that we will only take children up through the sixth grade."

Will and Caroline looked at each other and laughed.

"What's so funny?" asked the caseworker.

"Well, we were talking about this the other day. We realize that Troy will be going into the sixth grade pretty soon, and there's no way we will part with him. So we decided we would have you remove the restriction on age. At least as far as Troy is concerned. He's not easy, but he's really working with us all the time," Will explained.

"I can tell I'm leaving Andrella in good hands. She's lucky to have you," replied the caseworker.

Andrella began to cry in the nursery and Caroline went to the kitchen to prepare a bottle for her afternoon feeding. After a few more notes were taken and questions answered, the caseworker packed up her briefcase and Will walked with her to the front door. She glanced at a framed wall hanging by the door. A quotation from the Bible about taking care of "widows and orphans" had been cross-stitched under a scene of a child swinging in a garden. It occurred to her that she'd just seen this verse in action.

Send To | **Attachments**

LatimerPNG@sopac.org

Subject: Helping Blackwells

Chuck!

Thanks for checking back with me on the Blackwells. You are going beyond the call of duty to offer your trans-Pacific services re. Andrella. But since you offered, I'll give them your e-mail address.

I know they will have tons of questions about the care of this new baby. She definitely has her mother's cocaine addiction. Trust me, your offer will be taken advantage of. Since they know you and Laurie from the LOV, they won't just be sending e-mail to a stranger. I'll also assure them that you are a "real" doctor and all that stuff.

These folks are quiet, solid farming people. You don't hear much from them, but when you do, they are usually right in the middle of something good. I understand Will had some rough years growing up, but when he had to take over running his Dad's dairy farm, he straightened out in a big hurry. He's now the example of what a man should be, in my humble opinion.

And now, back to the ongoing saga of Jenny and Raleigh. There's more....the music swells.........

Bye for now,
Wayne

```
┌─ Send To ─┬─ Attachments ─┐
│                           │
│  ┌──────────────────────┐ │
│  │ Summit Meetings      │ │
│  └──────────────────────┘ │
└───────────────────────────┘
```

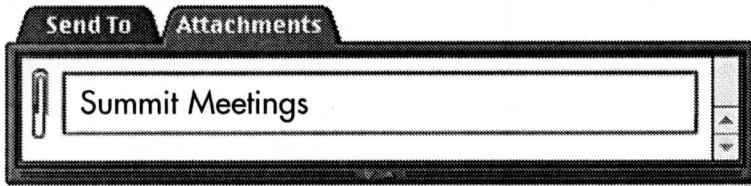

SUMMIT MEETINGS

Rosetta Lawrence descended the steps of the bus and began scanning the bus terminal for Raleigh. He and Dee Wight had purposely positioned themselves inside the building. Raleigh could read her mind: "Now where is that boy? I wonder if he had an accident? I can't believe he's late. I know I gave him my schedule!" They had a long history of loving each other intensely and at the same time struggling to get along about the details in life.

Finally she spotted them grinning at her through the window. They waved at her as soon as her glance came their way. She knew in an instant what they were up to.

"Now, Raleigh, don't be teasing me now," she said as she came through the door that Dee Wight was holding open for her. She had a big hug for both men. They could tell she had almost been in tears.

"Mama, don't you be upset. We were right here all the time. I didn't want to breathe all those bus fumes, so we waited inside," he fibbed. Dee Wight nudged him as Rosetta bustled on by them to go claim her luggage. She had two very heavy suitcases.

"How on earth could you pack so much on such short notice?" Raleigh complained as he carried out her luggage. He dearly loved to harass his mother.

"Well, I didn't know what we'd be doing or how long I'd be here, so I brought a little of everything. Most of that second suitcase is your baby clothes I've been saving. They were hand made by Zachary's great grandmother."

The three of them loaded themselves and all of Rosetta's treasures into Raleigh's car and drove off toward Dee Wight's boyhood home. The trip was short and simple, but the silence was long and tense. Finally, Rosetta started talking. She replayed all the questions she had asked Raleigh on the phone earlier in the day. Then she put Dee Wight on the spot.

"Well, Dee? What do you think about all this?"

Dee Wight was caught by surprise, but after choking on the cold drink he had bought at the bus station, he said, "Aunt Rosetta, I'm pretty sure this is all going to work out just fine." He was glad that his comment seemed to placate his aunt a bit. Raleigh shot him an appreciative glance.

The reunion out at the Smith's place was a happy one. The family rarely had opportunities to get together anymore. The chores for Dee Wight's dad were done easily by the two strong men. As soon as there was a reasonable time to break into the visit, Raleigh interrupted things by saying,

"I think I need to go over to the Dabneys and talk to Jenny. I know she is going to want to meet you, all of you. I'll see when we can set something up to all get together with her family and Zach." It didn't take long for him and Dee Wight to unload the luggage.

Raleigh planted a big kiss on Rosetta's cheek as they left and said, "Now, Mama, don't you worry. I'm going to get you a look at my baby boy as soon as I can. Just let me see how's best to work this all out."

Rosetta knew it would be awhile before Raleigh and Dee Wight showed up again at the farm. But, she was willing to wager her mother's hand made baby clothes that he would have her grandson and his mother with him when he arrived. So Rosetta decided they'd better start cooking at the Smith farm.

~~~~~~~~~~~~~~~

The next afternoon, a very nervous Raleigh pulled into the driveway at the Dabney residence. He and Jenny had talked a long time the night before over dessert and coffee at Lola's. Everything was planned ahead of time for the family get together at the Smiths' farm for supper.

Jenny, Chelsea, and Zachary were waiting on the front porch for him. Zachary was dressed in his bright red overalls, and ready for the big visit with his daddy and his grandmother. But he had been fussy all afternoon, and was still unhappy in his mother's arms. When Jenny carried him out to the car to meet Raleigh, she noticed that there were new age-appropriate child carriers in the back seat of the car. Chelsea, also dressed in her overalls for a visit to the farm, jumped into her seat with her usual armload of books and her favorite stuffed rabbit.

"Nice touch, Lieutenant. You really think of everything, don't you? The car seats are perfect," Jenny smiled her approval.

"You didn't think I'd be illegal with my little guy and his sister, did you?" he asked as he helped her buckle Zachary in the carseat for the drive out to his aunt and uncle's farm. Chelsea already knew how to fasten herself in.

"No, I just thought we'd have to use mine."

He reached over and brushed her cheek with the back of his fingers, "You're right. . . .when we're in your car, we will." He noted that she didn't pull away when he touched her. Good sign.

"Fine by me," she replied. "I just don't know how this visit is going to go with my being so jittery and Zachary so cranky. I hope he'll go to sleep for awhile on the way out."

"You'll all do just fine, Jenny. Rosetta will love it if she has to fuss with Zach. I'm sorry that I didn't have more time to prepare things for Mama's visit. She really did spring this on me yesterday morning when I called her about what's been going on. I'm probably more up tight than you are right now." They both laughed and felt more relaxed. Raleigh glanced in the rear-view mirror at Zachary and Chelsea.

"He's already about gone," Raleigh commented, and Jenny nodded in relief. She was fascinated by how things seemed to come together for her when Raleigh was around, just the opposite of what she would have expected. Chelsea was "reading" her books, which she knew by heart, to no one in particular. Raleigh turned onto the country road for the ride out to the Smiths' farm.

The scenery in front of them was spectacular and the air was clean and cool as they rode through the countryside. As they came to a scenic overlook, Raleigh pulled over to give them a better look at the setting sun. He opened the doors for Jenny and Chelsea to get out of the car. Zachary now dozed peacefully in the coming twilight. Chelsea jumped out, and began picking up rocks to throw over the edge of the overlook. Raleigh showed her how to throw one 'Up, Up and Awaaaaaay!'

He leaned up against the side of the car and pulled Jenny close to him. He had a lot to say, but he knew that they didn't have much time before they were expected for dinner. They both kept a watchful eye on Chelsea so that she didn't play too close to the overlook barrier or the road.

"Jenny, I know these last few days have been like a whirlwind for both of us. Can we talk a few minutes before we get my family too far into the mix?"

"Sounds like a good idea to me," replied a curious Jenny who felt the same. She had enjoyed Raleigh's visits and getting to know him better. And she had wondered when they'd talk about where their relationship was headed. She had thought she would probably have to bring up the subject. Her past boyfriends, including Chelsea's father, had backpedaled and never wanted her to be 'so serious' when she found enough courage to ask them questions about possible future commitments. "Go on."

"You know, I really prayed that God would help me find you again before I drove back into Little River. Like I told you that first night, I had such a strong sense of needing to get back to you, and for a long time I couldn't figure where that was coming from. But since I've been here with you and Zachary, I've had an even stronger feeling that God is at work in our relationship."

Jenny opened her mouth to reply, and Raleigh put his finger across her lips. "Now just be quiet for a few minutes. I want to be sure I say it all." With her blue-gray eyes locked into his, Jenny slowly nodded her assent.

"Zachary has just taken my heart away. And Chelsea is a total angel. To watch the three of you together these past few days is the biggest blessing I've ever had. You are just beautiful together, and you didn't need any help in that department."

He smiled, as he "shh'ed" her once again. By now, tears were slipping down Jenny's cheeks. He gave her his handkerchief and went on. Chelsea continued with her rock-throwing project.

"If you've wondered where I've spent my time here in Little River, a lot of it's been right here looking out over these hills and praying about you and me and these two children. There's a great limestone overhang down the hill a little ways that I want to show you when we have more time. God really met me down there. I've thrown more rocks over that cliff than I care to count. I don't want to rush you into anything. It's just....Jenny, I'm so sure. I love you so much."

By now, he was holding her close and she buried her face in his shoulder. "I don't know what you'll say about this, but Jenny, I want you to marry me. Let's make the four of us into the family I'm sure God wants us to be. I wanted to ask you before we get over to Rosetta and all the distraction with her and the baby and Chelsea and my family and all that stuff. This evening is going to get complicated in very short order. You know what I mean? OK? Please say 'yes?' I know this is pushing things."

He had run out of his carefully chosen words and planned proposal. He knew he was beginning to sputter. He slowly looked down and at her and waited for her answer.

At this moment Chelsea skipped over and said she needed to go to the bathroom, "really BAD!" She couldn't be dissuaded, so Jenny quickly took her over behind one of the roadside bushes. When they came back, Chelsea picked up more rocks and asked Raleigh to throw them for her while she squealed, "Up, Up, and Awaaaaaaay!" Jenny checked on Zachary, then went back to Raleigh's side, as she silently thanked God that the children were letting them talk.

"Somehow, I don't feel like this is a rushed thing, Raleigh. I told my Dad early on, even before Zachary arrived, that I wished you'd stayed in touch and that I thought you were a pretty great guy. I can't think of a thing that has changed my mind about that. A lot of the anger I felt has gone away." By now, Jenny was openly crying, but she managed to say into his strong embrace, "And there's a lot of love for you in its place."

Raleigh was still holding his breath and hanging onto Jenny. "Girl, I'm sorry, but if you don't answer my question pretty soon, I am going to roll right off this cliff."

"Oh, of course!" she looked up quickly. "Of course, it's 'Yes.' I thought you knew that when I started crying."

"Like I said a few days ago, you are the queen of the one word answers. But I do need to hear you say a 'yes.' That's all I wanted to hear."

Nodding, she turned her head to kiss him, but he said, "Wait, hold on just a minute." He reached into his jacket pocket and pulled out an engagement ring that he slipped onto her ring finger. The stone was big enough to catch the glow of the sunset.

"Oh, it's beautiful! But when did you get this, Raleigh?" She was astounded.

"I stopped on my way out to your house just now. In fact,

I made two stops, one for the car seats, and one for the ring. I want you to know that I am dead serious about reeling you and Zachary and Chelsea in beside me. And I wanted to see if you had an answer for me before we have to deal with Rosetta and all this falderol happening out at the farm."

"Well, you can relax. Please, tell me you don't have any more surprises for me. I don't think my heart can handle another one after this."

"No more for you, Jenny. But, now we get to surprise everyone else with our news." He went back to his explanation. "I don't know much about rings, but I know this one is pretty standard. Actually, Dee was along with me to help me out with my shopping. I want you to have any setting you want for the stone. The jeweler knows we may be back tomorrow. I even told him I might have to return the ring if you said, 'No.' "

"No way, Raleigh. Someone like you, a baby boy like Zachary, a little girl like Chelsea, and a ring exactly like this are what I've always wanted," she smiled and sniffled into his handkerchief.

"Now will you quit your talking and explaining and please kiss me?" She reached for his collar and pulled him to her. His knees felt weak with relief, and he was glad they were leaning against his refurbished Trans-Am. Chelsea finally came over and let them know she was getting bored. "Can we go to the farm now?"

As they continued down the road to the farm, Raleigh told her that he had made a call after he left the jeweler. He had talked to Vic Dabney. "I called him on his cell phone, and told him what I was planning to do. He said if you were agreeable, that he and your mom would give us their blessing. I even talked to Stella about it for a minute."

"What! They knew about this before I left?" She was amazed that they had kept the secret. Jenny went on to say that she was surprised her parents were agreeable because they usually did not approve of short engagements or rushed up marriages. She thought a minute and added, "I guess they must be making an exception due to our 'history' together? You think? Either that, or they know what a catch you are and are afraid I'll let you get away?" She looked at him with a silly grin. He reached over, took her hand and kissed the new ring on her finger.

"But, they know you have to leave the country soon, and that we have Zachary to think about. To me, it feels like things are coming together, not that they're rushed. We just put the cart before the horse, and now we have a chance to line things up like they should be." She smiled as she looked down at her engagement ring. "So I guess you made a good impression on Vic and Stella?"

"I guess so," Raleigh replied. "And they haven't even seen me in my uniform!" Jenny loved the way he made them laugh at each other.

"I guess you'll have to wear it for our wedding."

"You know, I hadn't even thought about what I'd wear. The army does try to make these things easy for us."

"I'll be the one in white," Jenny retorted.

As they came around the curve and down to the farmhouse, they could see people in the yard and picnic tables ready. Everyone was waving and waiting for Zachary and his entourage to arrive. As soon as the car rolled to a stop and Raleigh and Jenny got out, Uncle Dee reached in and took Zachary out of his new car seat.

Chelsea crawled out of the car and was suddenly shy around so many strangers. But that only lasted for a moment. There were plenty of children around. She was soon playing with her new friends, and showing them how to throw rocks with the proper vocal accompaniment. Raleigh introduced Jenny to Rosetta and showed her their new engagement ring. Rosetta began to act a little miffed that she didn't already know about the engagement until Jenny said,

"But, YOU are the very first person to know. This just happened on the way out here." Raleigh knew that his diplomatic fiancé had won his mother's heart with those words. He was pleased that this meeting of his two worlds was going so well.

Rosetta finally pried Zachary away from Uncle Dee Wight who'd been holding his nephew up above his head and out of her reach. "I knew if I didn't get a'hold of him first, I'd never get him at all. So now, he's all yours." Zachary stayed sound asleep in his adoring grandmother's arms.

As the picnic was breaking up, Jenny invited Raleigh and Rosetta over to the Dabney's for lunch the next day.

"I want you to come over so Rosetta can meet my family. And I guess we'll have to start planning a wedding, won't we?"

"Well, Honey," Rosetta interrupted her, "You just consider your wedding dress made. Bring me any pattern you like, and I'll have that dress ready before you know it."

Jenny looked over at Raleigh and said, "That's wonderful! But, Raleigh, we haven't even set a date?"

Raleigh replied, "That's simple, we either do it when I finish my training in Cleveland, or we do it a year from now when I have my next furlough?"

"You know, Rosetta," Jenny replied, "we better go shopping for wedding dress supplies tomorrow because there is no way I'm waiting a year to get married."

Raleigh wished that his buddy in Georgia could see this scene playing itself out in front of him. He would have to call him soon to collect his $100, and a lot of bragging rights. The tune playing in his head had changed from the "Doxology" of a few days ago to the "Hallelujah Chorus."

Send To	Attachments

LatimerPNG@sopac.org

Subject: Big Day in Little River

Hi, Chuck and Laurie.

It's times like these that make me miss you extra. Yesterday was the Lawrences' wedding day. It was such a special time for the community as well as the happy couple. So that everyone would feel welcome, Raleigh came up with the idea of having the wedding at the Gazebo on the Town Square. It was a bit chilly, but his idea worked like a charm. I'm sure there will be more weddings there as a result. It was wonderful to see members of both churches enjoy one another. God helped out with my nerves and He also gave us a beautiful day. Plan B was to move to the LOV church if the Gazebo plans got rained out.

Cayla is sitting here on my lap because I promised her she could tell you all about the wedding. She will dictate and I, her devoted secretary, will do the typing duties. Here goes:

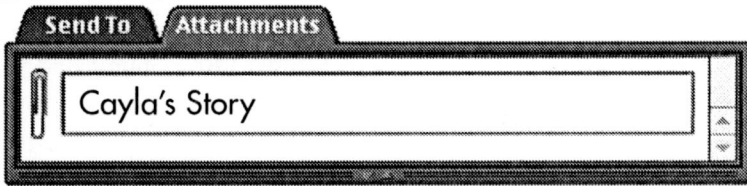

| Send To | Attachments |

Cayla's Story

CAYLA'S STORY

This weekend I was in my very first wedding. I gave programs to people who came to the wedding. I wore a long pink dress my mom made. It matched everyone else's pink dress. It is my first long dress, and I like it a lot. My daddy says I look pretty in it.

The bride was Jenny Dabney and the groom was Raleigh Lawrence. Jenny's father, Uncle Vic, walked with Jenny up to where Raleigh was standing. She wore a pretty white dress that Raleigh's mother made for her. He wore his soldier's uniform, sort of like those G. I. Joe dolls, only fancier.

Jenny's sister, Darcy, was the maid of honor, and Dee Wight Smith, Raleigh's cousin, was the best man. Dee Wight is the biggest man in Little River. Darcy wore a pink dress that her mom made. It's just like mine. She is my friend, but she's a lot older than I am.

Chelsea, Jenny's little girl, was the flower girl, and she wore a pink dress too. Zachary came to the wedding in a little wooden wagon that Uncle Vic made for him. Zachary did not wear pink because baby boys don't wear pink. Darcy wanted Raleigh to wear a pink shirt so he would match better, but he said the army wouldn't let him do that with his uniform.

The wedding was downtown at the Gazebo. That's the big porch place where those bands come and play music in the summer. No one can remember anyone ever having a wedding there before. Daddy spent a long time talking in the Gazebo about that getting married stuff, and then Raleigh and Jenny gave each other real pretty rings. Dee Wight and Darcy showed them to me before the wedding. They had to carry the rings for Raleigh and Jenny up to the Gazebo, but I'm not sure why because they weren't very heavy. After they gave each other the rings, Daddy talked some more, and then told them they had to kiss. I mean, you know, just Raleigh and Jenny kissed…kinda long. Then we could eat.

The wedding cake was the biggest, tallest cake you can ever imagine. It had these cute little dolls on top that looked just like Jenny and Raleigh. Zachary was too little to eat cake, but Chelsea ate some and dropped it all over her pink dress. I had fun, but I ate too much cake and had a stomach ache last night.

Oh, they had this awesome pink punch in these pretty plastic cups. Joshua and I tried to see how many empty cups we could find, and we gathered a stack of them as tall as I am. Mom wouldn't let us bring even one of them home. She told us to mind our manners.

Raleigh and Jenny have gone on their honeymoon for three days, and we are baby sitting Zachary and Chelsea for Stella during the day since she has to work or something. I have fun playing with them. When Raleigh and Jenny get back, we have to help them pack up because they are going to live in some place across the ocean.

OK, that's all. Oh, my Dad just said that the new Lawrences will be living across a different ocean than yours.

Bye, I miss you!
Cayla.

P. S. So now you have the news straight from one who was a witness of every, trust me, EVERY detail! Cute kid, that Cayla. She didn't stick around long after she gave me her version of the wedding.

We'll fill in more details later, and will put the photos

Trudy took out there on the LOV web-site for you to enjoy. So many people asked about you. I'm just sorry Dr. Chuck Inc. couldn't be here.

Trudy's been shopping for you guys for Christmas already. She says we need to get it all in the mail this month because it takes forever to arrive half way around the world.

W.L.

THE NEXT SPRING

Send To **Attachments**

LatimerPNG@sopac.org

Subject: Recovery

Helloooooo!

This is my first attempt at typing since they took the cast off my hand. I'm sure there will be many typos. Thank God for 'spell- check' and all other word processing gifts.

It's been eons since I last wrote to you guys over there. With all the holidays, I guess there was just no time to write down any LOV stories. I'm glad that Trudy and Laurie have sort of kept everyone up on the essentials via snail mail. I guess you heard that after Christmas we all had that bad flu that everyone was passing around?

Suffice it to say, I already owed you an e-mail from way back before life changed forever on Easter Sunday. A thousand pardons. It seems banal to say, "Lots has happened."

Speaking of gifts, your surprise visit was a true gift right out of heaven. I could NOT believe it when I opened my eyes and there you were. Of course, at the time I did not know I had been in a coma for 10 days. To wake up in a hospital room was surreal.

Also, thanks to Laurie and the kids. She was quite a trooper to send you home for awhile. We seriously needed your presence, Bud. It helped so many LOV folks to have you here as a medical sounding board.

I am just beginning to piece things together in my head. I am trying to figure out what happened. You know I'll write all this down when my hands (and my head) loosen up. I'm really anxious to tell my story before the memory fades too much.

For now, I'm just happy to be all in one piece. Trudy and I make quite a pair trying to take care of each other "in sickness and in health." At least we're alive, at home, and mending together. We're pretty clumsy...mostly funny. Is this what people call a "bonding experience?" Right now she's talking about weeding out all our old files while we are home together. What is it with this woman? At least I know she's feeling better when she comes up with a new project like this file thing.

The children have been super to help out and try to keep things going around here. We are finding out that they are capable in ways we never dreamed. Wonder of wonders, they even help each other out a lot.

We're slowly recovering. I know, however, we will never be the same. So many have lost so much. My flock is hurting. So am I. A wonderful sidebar to all this: there has never been a moment when I have not felt God's presence with me. He has surrounded me with His love and comfort. It's palpable.

I am more motivated than ever to get out of the way, and let Jesus accomplish His work through me. I know that He will somehow use this painful experience in the life of our church family. That thought makes rehab and recuperation worthwhile. I want to get healthy so I can watch this happen!

My account of the Easter events follows. See if my memories match up with what you know about it all.

Pray for us lots.......
Wayne

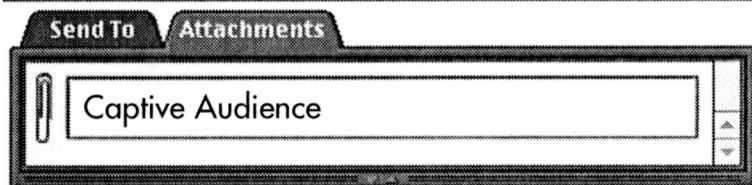

Captive Audience

CAPTIVE AUDIENCE

The Easter Sunday worship service was always Trudy's favorite. In her mind it was her payback for all the times she felt left out of Wayne's life and ministry. It gave her a fresh connection to what her role as a pastor's wife was all about.

After all, she had known about Wayne's plans to be a minister from their very first date. She had decided she wanted the whole package, and she had never regretted her decision. She did sometimes feel lost in the shuffle of other people's problems and programs. But Easter Sunday was hers.

This Easter, she was again ready and waiting in the wings before the celebration of the resurrection began. And, as in years past, she and Wayne were dressed up in Biblical-era costumes, ready to act out a drama for the Easter service. The reason for Trudy's close connection to this particular annual service was that she always wrote and staged the drama. Another incidental fact: she always starred in her dramas. Somehow each year the drama was a litmus test for her own faith in the risen Christ.

It was interesting how each year scripted it's own drama. The year they adopted their first child, Cayla, the play was a conversation between John and Mary as they left the crucifixion as a newly adoptive mother and son. Another year, after she had been in charge of the mission week supper for a huge crowd, she wrote all about an imaginary woman who prepared the Last Supper.

This year, she thought she had written the best of her dramas. She and Wayne were going to be the two disciples on the way back to Emmaus after the resurrection of Jesus. In the drama she was going to ask all of her own questions as a part of the conversation along the road.

Trudy was well known for coming up with searching questions about Christianity; in fact, that is how she and Wayne first became acquainted. She had gone on a college class church retreat and had met Wayne over a campfire with hot dogs and s'mores. Their conversation lasted until the fire died down, and the other campers had turned in. They talked and talked. Trudy had finally found someone who was interested in listening to all her questions. Wayne, then a pre-ministerial student, was very pleased that he could answer a few of her most intense queries, and flirt with such a pretty freshman girl at the same time.

The congregation of the Lily of the Valley Community Church was slowly gathering. There was the usual fluffing of Easter dresses, crowded seating, and the hushed anticipation of the coming drama. Babies cried, and everyone else whispered. The worship team was playing inspiring music that ignited everyone's thinking about the resurrection.

The worshippers had brought in fresh flowers from their spring gardens and placed them on a huge cross that was molded from chicken wire. The wire was now almost completely covered with a beautiful blanket of flowers.

Making this cross was Wayne's project the first Easter they were in the ministry. He'd read about this tradition in an old novel about a country preacher, and now it was a tradition he looked forward to each year. The local newspaper even sent out a photographer last year, and the flower covered cross was on the front page of that Monday's edition.

Trudy and Wayne were finally ready for their big moment. They rehearsed their lines one more time in Wayne's office just down the hall from the worship center. He looked nervously into the hall as he heard the music swell with the songs of Easter.

How are we doing?" asked Trudy, meaning, "I wonder how full the auditorium is?" Then she went on, "I always get nervous about no one showing up for these things."

Wayne smiled down at her and adjusted her headpiece. "You know you'll have a captive audience on Easter Sunday, Trudy, so not to worry." He loved to tease her when she was nervous, which only made her more nervous.

"Thanks a bunch, Padre," Trudy nudged him as she now looked out and down the hall.

"I'd be more worried about you if you flipped over and got over confident on me," Wayne quipped back. "You just say the word and we can go to having a sunrise service like every other church on the planet."

"Come on," whispered an usher as he leaned inside the door and gave them their cue to be ready.

As they rustled down the short hall toward the auditorium, Trudy made a handshake deal with Wayne, "Just for the record, I'll keep these masterpieces coming as long as God keeps giving me the ideas."

"OK, OK, it's a deal. Don't be so defensive," said Wayne as he peeked through a little concealed window into the now full auditorium. "I'll be," he whispered, "you won't believe who's here?"

"I give," said Trudy after she tried to stand on her tiptoes to see through the tiny window. "Tell me!" She had to keep adjusting her headpiece.

"Donny Transome! Jennifer never thought he'd ever again darken the doors of this church, or for that matter any other church."

"But when was he released from Slocum?" asked Trudy with a touch of alarm in her voice.

"He must've worked out something with his parole board again. Maybe he's decided to turn over a new leaf."

"Don't hold your breath, Wayne. I doubt he's changed much. Jennifer told me some downright scary stories about him. I'm glad she and Raleigh are in Europe or she'd be extremely nervous about his being here. Maybe he came here looking for Chelsea? Surely he knows they've left."

"SHHH, two more bars, then everyone sings 'Christ the Lord Is Risen Today,' and we're on." Now Wayne focused on his congregation and Rev. and Mrs. Latimer's part in making this a meaningful Easter morning for everyone.

Trudy was gazing out the window in the hallway. The morning was glowing. It was her favorite time of the day even before it became an Easter morning.

Simultaneously, things happened.

There was the deafening roar of an explosion. Wayne was on top of her and hurting her. The glowing morning vanished and the music ceased. Amidst the sound of the chandeliers from the ceiling of the worship center crashing to the floor, Trudy lost consciousness.

Soon sirens began wailing in the distance. The moans of the injured, the shouts of survivors turned rescuers, and the cries of frightened children were all that remained of the captive audience that Trudy was counting on. A few crumpled blossoms dangled from the wire cross that lay twisted and broken at the front of the church.

Donny Transome was no more. His tormented life ended in a shower of explosives, as he ignited his simple but powerful bomb. It had been strapped to his chest under a bulky jacket, one that had seemed unseasonably heavy for an Easter morning.

A dense cloud of dusty smoke settled over the town of Little River. It floated down into the valleys and spread along every street. The choking atmosphere was slowly dispersed by a gentle breeze on what should have been a lovely Easter Sunday. That evening a lavender overlay remained on the horizon as a full moon rose over the smoldering site where the Lily of the Valley Community Church once stood.

Send To **Attachments**

LatimerPNG@sopac.org

Subject: Apology

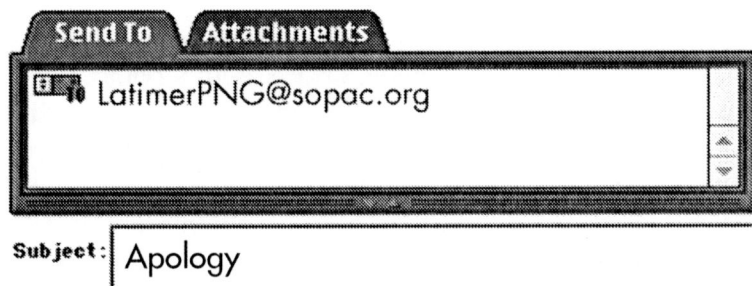

Hi, Chuck and Laurie and kids,

Yes, I realize that I left the story unfinished. I have to apologize for not writing more about what happened after the Easter Sunday tragedy. But there was a reason.

After I wrote about the events of that morning, I went into a major depression for awhile. All I could do was cry for about twenty-four hours. I guess I really scared some of the folks here, especially Trudy. The conclusion we all came to was that I wasn't ready to re-live that day, even if it was only on paper. I'm told I am a textbook case of Post-Traumatic Stress Disorder. Stef has been great. He suggested both Trudy and I take some medication for depression and PTSD. The Rx was hard to get used to, but it has really helped.

Stef offered to tell me his side of the Easter morning. He said it would help him to think it all through, and it would help me to hear someone else's account of that day. That way, it won't be so personal to me. Also, he said he thought I still needed to wait awhile.

Finally, we've found a time that's good for both of us, and now I am trying to put it all on the word processor. He's coming over tonight to help me finish it out and to be sure the details are straight. It is helping us both heal to work on this together. He keeps reminding me that he saved my life, but I don't remember it!

Everyone continues to recover in increments. I hurt for

Stella Dabney. She's having a hard time navigating with crutches. I'm glad that Jenny and Raleigh could come home for Vic's funeral. I guess the army understands what people go through in this sort of situation. After all, it was an incendiary device.

Ms. Demarco is remarkable. You remember she had that major head injury, but she laughs it off now that she is up and around. She brought a latte and a piece of pie to me the other day, and said I was not to worry about her. "Even before this happened, people thought I'd bumped my head." She is some kind of character. Her injuries left her with major scars, but they will fade in time.

The plans for a new church are going nowhere. Right now, no one wants to rebuild on the sight of the old church, so we are looking for a solution to that dilemma. Meanwhile, we're sharing the building of the Galilee Valley Church. They meet in the afternoon, and let us use their building on Sunday mornings. They've really reached out to us.

I'll try to do better with the e-mail. I'll keep you posted. Take care....

Love to all 4,
Wayne

P.S. Dr. Chuck: OK, before I hear from you PDQ....don't freak out about the depression I just told you about. We have a great God and a fabulous support system here. Both are fully operational! I wanted to be up front about what is happening around the LOV parsonage as I promised you I would when you left.

And, you did warn me to expect more than just a physical recovery period. I am very thankful for your words of wisdom, because when my emotions took a dive, I was not nearly so fearful as I might have been. At least I knew that it was not unusual to own those kinds of feelings and fears after an experience like ours.

Once again, thanks for your part in our recovery. You are a brother in every sense of the word.

W.L.

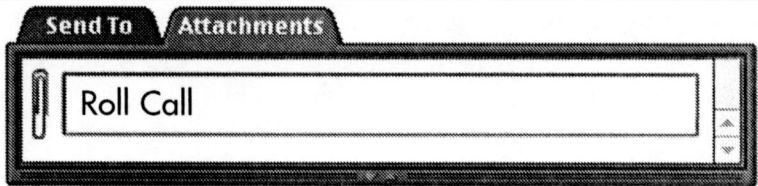

Roll Call

ROLL CALL

At Riverton General Hospital, Dr. Stefan Gentry had swiftly set up triage care for the injured as they were brought into the Emergency Room. He had to steel his emotions and shut his mind to the horrific realization that the rushing, wailing ambulances along with people in private vehicles were all coming from the Lily of the Valley Community Church. His own church!

Bits and pieces of information came along with the paramedics as they arrived from the scene of the disaster. All Dr. Gentry could piece together in the midst of the confusion was that the explosion he had heard earlier in the distance had occurred in the Lily of the Valley Community Church's worship center as the Easter church service was beginning. No one seemed to know what had caused the explosion. There was a possibility of an underground gas leak, but the police at the scene were saying it was most likely a bomb. No one knew much at all at this point. The injured worshippers were everyone's main concern.

He found out from an ambulance driver that the church's education wing seemed to be unharmed by the blast. He assumed for the moment that his bride, Ellen, who was helping as an extra volunteer in the crowded nursery, was safe. With that small bit of reassurance, he was able to focus on what he needed to do as the senior physician of the moment at Riverton General.

He had been making his morning rounds when his beeper had paged him. When he answered the page, he was ordered

STAT to the Emergency Room. The ER supervisor was telling him than an emergency had been brought in by private vehicle, and several more injuries were on their way by ambulance. He was urged to hurry.

Stefan ran down several flights of stairs rather than wait on the sluggish elevator. Everyone had heard the explosion in the distance, so he supposed there were injuries from some sort of a blast. He tried to mentally steel himself for what he might find in the ER, but in retrospect, there was no way to prepare for what was waiting for him.

"Wayne, can you hear me?" Stefan asked as the blood soaked gurney was rolled from the ambulance and into the ER. When there was a flicker of response, Stefan squeezed his pastor's shoulder, and whispered, "Hold on, Wayne. It's Stef. We're going to pull you and Trudy through this just fine. We're not sure what caused the explosion. Everyone's working real hard to take care of people right now. You just relax, and let us take over." He hoped his voice sounded confident.

He quickly gave the nurse beside him a few basic details about Wayne Latimer. She filled him in on other details, "That ambulance that arrived first brought in a Mrs. Latimer. Must be this man's wife?" Stefan nodded with a quizzical expression for her to go on.

"She has major injuries to her lower back and legs. Someone else admitted her, so that's all I can tell you." Then she pulled the curtain around the threesome in the cubicle and began to cut Wayne's elaborate head covering away from his wounds.

"Let's get Rev. Latimer stabilized and on his way to the OR. He is the pastor of the church where this explosion went off. He's thirty-five years old. Page the neuro-surgeon on call. He may already be en route if he's heard about all this," he said to the nurse. She was frantically scribbling his instructions on a metal chart. "While you're on the phone, get the main desk to put out a call to all the docs on our roster. Tell them to get over here ASAP. I think we're going to need them."

Wayne had passed into unconsciousness as soon as he heard his life-long friend's voice. At least he knew that Trudy was alive. Stefan did not want to leave Wayne, but another ambulance had just arrived. He wiped his hand over his brow as he removed his gloves and pitched them into the wastebin. "This man is one of my best friends." The nurse winced and shook her head.

As Stefan watched the next ambulance arrive to be unloaded, he thought fleetingly of his father, "Dr. Max," now in full retirement. "Who said you could skip this one, Maxwell Gentry?" he muttered. He knew that the news of the disaster would soon reach his father at the nursing home. He assumed that right now his dad and Lida were holding hands and drinking coffee under the ficus trees in the solarium. It was almost time for them to be singing "The Old Rugged Cross" as a visiting parson played on an auto-harp for their Easter service.

Stefan slipped quickly into fresh gloves, and recoiled as the next gurney was rolled in. The patient was totally covered. The attendant pulled back the sheet for a moment, and the still, white face of Vic Dabney was revealed. After a moment to assess Vic's condition he spoke softly to the nurse standing by, "No vital signs. This is Vic Dabney. Time of death: 11:10."

Inwardly, he shuddered. He was thinking of Jennifer and Raleigh and the shattering news they would shortly receive half way around the world. And he wondered briefly where Stella and Darcy were?

"God, what on earth happened out there to my friends and my church?" Weeping, he left the triage scene briefly before the next ambulance arrived. He could hear it in the distance. He went to the break room just long enough to pull himself together.

He reached for the coffeepot and noticed that he was holding the handle in a vice-like grip. He momentarily upbraided himself for not eating a decent breakfast before he rushed out of the house that morning. Rushing on over to church for the Easter drama had been his main agenda. He had become quite impatient when several talkative patients with lots of questions had delayed him. He realized now that he was possibly alive because of those questions.

Now he was the one with the Easter morning questions, and he was suddenly a player in the Little River Easter Drama. He knew it was going to be a very long day. He took a deep breath and re-entered the triage scene at Riverton General Hospital.

A little girl with a crumpled Easter basket sat all alone in the ER waiting room. "Thank God, here's at least one who isn't hurt," he thought as he walked over to the little girl to reassure her. She was very quiet, and stared at him with bewilderment in her enormous blue eyes. He motioned for one of the nurses.

"Let's find a place where this little gal can feel more secure. She's pretty traumatized. Maybe she could go up to the pediatric playroom? Be sure to put her name on her dress and also let me have it over at the main desk. See if she knows who brought her in." He did not want her to witness all that he knew would be coming through the emergency entrance of Riverton General Hospital. As he walked over to the triage desk, he found no answers to his inquiries about the little girl's parents.

He turned his attention to the next emergency arriving through the automatic doors. The sound of a life flight helicopter descending onto the hospital helipad dominated all other sound. An ambulance was being unloaded. He wondered who would be next?

Sam Loftis was brought in on the next gurney. Nora was with him. They had been greeting latecomers at the back door of the church, and both were unhurt except for a few bruises. But, Sam was having chest pains. Nora needed some medication to help her calm down, and Sam was admitted for a complete cardiatric work-up later in the day. They had driven over from Lakeland County for the Easter Service. Both were frantic because they hadn't seen Joel.

It wasn't long before Joel Loftis and Jill Sinclair walked in together. Everyone was relieved to hear that the massive explosion had missed the Significant Singles classroom. Their class had been late letting out, so everyone from that class was spared the nightmare in the main auditorium. Joel and Jill had been discussing the joys and sorrows of teaching together at the Little River High School when the force of the explosion knocked everyone in the room to the floor.

After everyone hugged each other with relief, Sam was lucid enough to tease Jill about her unusual tactics for picking up men. Joel blushed more than Jill did, and both dodged Sam's remarks.

The next helicopter brought in Isabella Demarco with severe lacerations and scalp wounds. She told Stefan to leave her alone and go help someone who really needed his help. He realized she meant it, so he went on to the next case. But he didn't let her wait for attention very long. As he introduced her to the plastic surgeon who would be treating her, she told them the helicopter ride was worth all the injuries. She made everyone smile when she said, "This proves it. There's no free ride to anywhere. Look at all this blood!"

Eva Souter, Frank's wife, was another of those who arrived completely covered and with no vital signs. Frank was admitted later via helicopter with a collapsed lung and a broken leg. One of the beams falling across the expanse of the worship center had taken Eva's life and seriously injured Frank. Eva's carefully prepared dishes for an Easter pot luck with the Dabneys were sitting unnoticed on the back seat of their car out in the newly paved church parking lot.

Caroline and Will's foster kids needed attention for some minor injuries, and then everyone was released but Andrella. Earlier that morning, the Blackwells had decided that the whole family would sit together because Andrella could not be left in the church nursery yet. No one in the nursery had the necessary training with the monitor. They decided it was best to sit on the very last row with their noisy brood. The outside walls of the church held up enough of the structure to protect them when the blast took out the roof of the church. The paramedics had insisted that Andrella be checked out due to her fragile health, so the whole family drove to the hospital with Andrella.

Stefan sent Andrella up to pediatrics for observation. He noticed that Troy never left Andrella's side. Stefan was always impressed with how much this foster family genuinely cared for each other. He knew that Caroline and Will were the secret ingredients that made it all happen.

Throughout that afternoon and evening, the citizens of Little River came by to help their friends and family. A long line of blood donors formed at the blood center across the street from Riverton General Hospital. The count of people who lost their lives rose throughout the day and into the evening. Several people who had survived were still in the ER or ICU, and some were not expected to survive.

The surgeons were working with very little rest between cases. Equipment and supplies from other hospitals had been hastily brought in to meet the demands of the disaster. Calls from all over the area had come in from physicians and medical personnel who were willing to help.

In the late evening, Ellen brought Stefan a hug and a carry-out meal from Lola's Café. He didn't know when he'd been so glad to see someone come through the ER doors and ask for him. He realized he was famished and quickly ate three or four bites out of the container as he stood talking to

Ellen. He handed the rest of the meal to one of the staff with a request to put it in the refrigerator in the doctors' lounge for him. The hospital staff was pleased to hear that Lola herself was catering a big delivery of food to help ease the pressures on the hospital cafeteria.

Ellen shared with him some especially good news. Ed and EmmaLu Sparks had gone on a retreat over Easter with the combined junior high and high school groups. They had taken quite a large group of teens up to the campground near the Lakeland County Pavilion. They'd planned to return Sunday night. Thus, most of the LOV young people were safe and sound, but had not yet learned of the disaster.

Because the Sparks' cell phone wasn't working, Pearle and JoLena were driving up to the Pavilion campground to tell the Sparks the news and to help them bring the campers home. Pearle and JoLena had the sad task of telling several of the children about the disaster's toll on their families. At last Pearle and JoLena had found a project they could work on without fighting.

Before Ellen left, he told her about the little girl in the waiting room, and asked her to go upstairs to Pediatrics to see if she was doing all right. He also asked her if anyone had thought to call his twin sister, Megan.

"Would you believe, she called me on my cell phone about 30 minutes after the explosion? I was still at the church nursery. I guess this tragic Easter story is already big news around the USA. Megan said the news came over her wire at the TV station just a few seconds before she called me. She said for you to prepare for a big interview by her and her TV crew sometime soon. Imagine that!"

"Great," grimaced Stef. He looked down at his bloody scrubs and said, "That's all I need." He gave Ellen a quick kiss and a long hug goodbye as one of the nurses waved him over to the triage center desk. "I gotta go," and he went back to work.

Send To	Attachments

To LatimerPNG@sopac.org

Subject: LOV Update

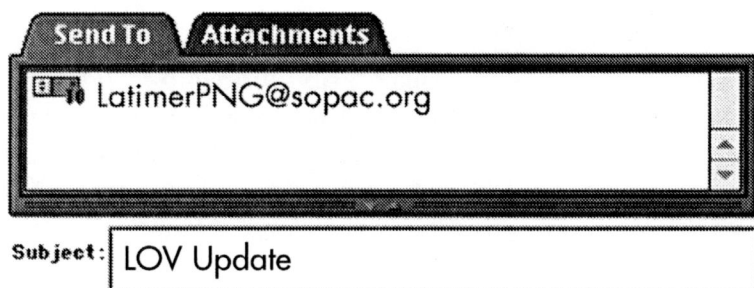

Hi, just thought I would update you two on how the LOV "recovery phase" is coming along. It has been amazing to see people team up to help one another.

Today, I heard from Ike Grant, who was willing to come back here to help out, but we decided to decline his offer for obvious reasons. There are too many people who are still struggling with what he did with their finances. Also, I'm not sure what his status is with the law enforcement people. When we have any sort of public acknowledgement of people and groups who have been helpful, I will be sure to mention his offer. On second thought, maybe not?

Dee Wight and other friends from Galilee Valley Church have come right along side. Their preacher has been a rock for all of us. He's done several funerals, met with families, and just been available whenever I've needed him.

Dee Wight has been totally supportive. He'd known Donny Transome over at the prison, and had spent quite a bit of time with him, so he has been wiped out over all this. He's taking a leave of absence from Slocum Prison to help clean up all the destruction. I think they have made him the Honorary Foreman on the job. Somewhere along the line he learned how to handle big equipment, so he has been invaluable. He usually stops in here daily and asks what we need.

Something amazing is going on in Dee Wight's heart. The other day he was grousing about having to go back to work at Slocum pretty soon. I guess prison life has been wearing on him. I asked him what he'd always dreamed of doing with his life. He said he'd always wanted to preach, but didn't have the money or the time to make it happen.

Let me tell you, I nearly flipped when he said that because someone had slipped me a tape of a Bible Study he has led over at Slocum for about a year. His teaching is awesome. So I was able to tell him that I think he has some gifts in that area. He was definitely surprised to hear that from me.

Bottom line is, Dee Wight and I are going to meet with Ed Sparks on a regular basis and pray about his future. Surely there's a school out there for him? He loves God's Word so much, and has such a heart for people. Now, won't that be something if he goes from prison guard to preacher? Sounds almost like something out of the New Testament here, don't you think?

Another interesting factoid: If Dee Wight becomes a preacher, 1/4 of the starting lineup of our highschool district championship team will be in the ministry. At least it will be if my being the team water boy counts for membership? Who but God could have taken our bunch of dirt bags this far? Well, I guess He is already on record with scruffy fishermen.

Did you remember that Ed is taking a Bible School degree by extension? He started working years ago on this degree, and had let it slide. I guess the experience last Easter helped him straighten out his priorities. EmmaLu may get to be married to a preacher after all.

Since Pearle and JoLena passed the peace pipe, they were asked to notify relatives and co-ordinate all the funeral arrangements that needed to be made. They have done an outstanding job, and are so proud of themselves for doing it all without fighting.

I think these two women are my Euodia and Syntche, the famous dueling ladies from Philippians 4:2. One day I took them aside and talked to them about Romans 12:16 where it says to "live in harmony," and down in vs. 18 where it says to "live at peace with everybody, as far as it depends on you." They kind of looked at each other and smiled when I said that living in harmony assumes people will play different notes. If they don't do things differently from each other, there's no harmony. If everyone is the same, then there is no song in life, only a monotone. It will sure help me to have them get along better in committee meetings. Those ladies really know how to annoy each other...and me.

There are still some things I can't do because I get so dizzy. Now don't get "diagnostic" on me, Doc. I am truly much better as long as I don't over do. The same goes for Trudy. She is moving around almost like her old self, but can't put in a full day yet. I think I'll be ready to preach again in a few weeks.

Some really sad news, Donny Transome's parents have split up. Mrs. Transome came by to talk the other day. I guess all their grief over Donny and what he did was the last straw for their marriage. One day after Easter, Mr. Transome just lost it and tore up their whole apartment. After that, Mrs. Transome said that she knew it was time to "split the blanket." She has put up with his temperamental behavior and alcoholism for years. He has been a very abusive man to her and their children. She's been going to counseling for some time and is now in an Al-Anon group. I think she is going to survive, but this whole tragedy will haunt her for the rest of her life.

Thank goodness, Jesus comforts us when we grieve. "Blessed are those that mourn, for they shall be comforted." What a gift He gives us in that process. At least, Donny's mother can move forward now without an abusive marriage hanging around her neck. She asked me what I thought people would say if she started attending the LOV Church again. I told her it would be a dose of healing medicine if she would return. I also told her to let me know when she was coming, and I would ask a couple of our women to be with her all the time. I am so privileged to assist a lost sheep back to safety. I know why David loved being a shepherd.

I knew that Donny was troubled, but I never thought he was dangerous. Everyone in Little River is saying the same thing. Lots of us have reached out to him at some point in his life, but he never wanted anything to do with me or with the folks at the LOV Church. His doctors from that rehab center have come over here to meet with some of us to help us understand what happens to a man with Donny's psychiatric profile. Trust me, we've needed all the help we can find on that topic. Looks like he was a true sociopath.

I don't think I've told you that Riverton General Hospital has been sending a team of counselors and specialists over to help us all deal with PTSD. They are amazed at how well we are doing, and how everyone has pulled together to help each other. It's not that we aren't in a lot of pain as a church family, but the support of the community of believers is a strong prescription for healing up from all this.

I never thought I'd say this, but it is fortunate in a way that I was knocked unconscious because I don't have all the visual memories to deal with. Suffice it to say, we're all doing better, but the memories and losses are still pretty fresh. At least Trudy doesn't have to write another Easter drama for next year.

With Ms. Demarco leading the worship this past

month there has really been a different spin on things. More on that later.

Write when you can get a minute between vaccinations and ear infections! Also, FYI, Mom and Dad recently said that they hadn't heard from you in a long time.

Yours,
Wayne

Send To **Attachments**

LatimerPNG@sopac.org

Subject: Pulpit Supply

CHARLES!!

OK! CHILL! Don't totally freak out on me. In the first place, Ms. Demarco is hardly a bonafide preacher. At her age, her voice is too weak even though her message is totally clear. With all the wires and amplifiers for her voice, we have been able to give her voice the boost it needs. But there's not a lot of future here in this scenario.

In the second place, we've received lots of good comments about letting her "supply" while I'm recovering. Someone even told me that her jokes are better than mine. That really hurt. I think having a female in the pulpit makes everyone feel very cosmopolitan. She has a true gift for distilling the tough passages down to something everyone can understand. The truth is there in an accessible form.

In the third place, it has been quite a challenge to cover all the LOV bases with so many of the church leadership people down and out these days. We've set up temporary quarters in a trailer that Frank Souter donated. We've had several new folks help out, but we've pretty well exhausted our resources by now. I'm working on setting up Dee Wight to preach for me one Sunday. He might as well begin with friends and see if he really does want to preach.

So.....bear with us in our pulpit supply struggles.

Back to Ms. Demarco. The reason you don't know

about her qualifications is simple: There aren't any in the official sense. None of us really knows the details of her past very well. She is such a recluse, you know. The stories, "Bully Pulpit" and "Coming Out" (which I will now endeavor to write, over her protests), will follow shortly. They will explain everything. Or at least as much as she will tell me.

The second story was written on one of our first chats after Easter. She was my first home visit after the doctors gave me the green light on resuming my activities. Things are busy, so don't fret if it takes awhile to get Ms. Demarco's story finished up and on its e-mail journey.

Before I sign off, I have a request. Look up some of those booklets by the elusive R. Shackleford Fuqua that we boxed and sent along with you over there. I think I may have tracked him down! Remember when we were trying to find him when Pastor Ike and Dad were reading everything by Fuqua that they could get their hands on? I'm still working on the trail to this gent, but it's warm. Looks like I'm getting close. Just call me "Super Sleuth/Snoop."

Blessings,
Wayne

```
Send To   Attachments

Bully Pulpit
```

BULLY PULPIT

Isabella walked from the kitchen back to her grandfather's room with a tray of black coffee and a piece of toast browned just as much as he liked it. This was her ritual every day with her beloved grandfather whenever her parents were gone. This meant every afternoon after his daytime companion left, most of the weekends, and all day everyday in the summer.

"I'm coming, Grandaddy," she called as she turned the corner from the kitchen down to his room.

"Good, sweetheart! You know you make the best toast in this whole town, don't you?"

"I hope so. And, the new journal from your seminary just came. Do you want me to read it to you?"

"Only after we finish our snack," he said as he savored the smells and tastes that she had brought with her into the room. Since he had lost his sight to glaucoma, his other senses had become much more important to him. But nothing was as dear to him as this precious granddaughter.

"I think I like this magazine better than all the others you get, Grandaddy. It isn't so hard to understand," she commented as she flipped through the pages. She read his journals and correspondence to him every day as part of their regular routine. In time, she had acquired an amazing knowledge and no small hunger for her grandfather's field of interest.

"I will never know why you try so hard to understand theology, Isabella. Wouldn't you rather be reading Nancy Drew or listening to the radio?" He was truly puzzled by this inquisitive young girl who was approaching womanhood. He reached over and touched her hair, knowing it was just like her grandmother's. A calm expression passed over his face as he was taken back into his own history by that touch.

"You know this is where I love to be and what I love to talk about. I want to learn about every book on these shelves," she reassured him as she gazed at the books that lined the walls of her grandfather's study.

"You do have a thirst for it! You remind me of when I was called to the ministry. But I don't know what to do with a talented girl who has that same hunger for the Word and all these textbooks."

"You'll just have to put up with me, I guess!"

II

And put up with her he did. Isabella pushed herself to learn what was in her grandfather's books and files. He was delighted to have someone eager to learn the same knowledge he had gained over the years. He had not been able to use it in any significant way since his eyesight had failed and forced his retirement. He was comforted by the memory that he had enjoyed a career as both a professor and a minister.

Fortunately, he still had his photographic memory, which was one of the keys to helping Isabella. He could send her all over his bookshelves and tell her on what page and in what paragraph to look for the needed explanation of a difficult passage. As she grew older, she became his secretary and research assistant. As much as he enjoyed having such a willing student and helper, he also puzzled over what she could do with her future. She was so talented and articulate, and now that she was almost out of college, he was even more impressed with her knowledge.

Isabella surprised him for his eighty-fifth birthday with

some writing she had done. She typed it up and turned it into a pamphlet for him so he could hold it in his hands while she read it to him.

"Bell, you are truly gifted as a writer! Do you know that?" he asked when she finished reading.

"You're just partial to me because I have curls like my Grandma's." she was teasing him now.

"No, I mean this very seriously. Now what are you planning to do with this writing of yours?" He waved the pamphlet toward the sound of her voice. "This is too good to just file away. I insist you do some serious thinking and praying about this."

"Well, Grandaddy, I guess God will have to show us what to do. All I have tried to do is write so difficult topics and themes are simple enough for us all to understand. I remember how you used to explain things to me when I was beginning to read the books in this room. I think more people would love the Bible if they could study it like you and I do. It doesn't have to be dull and boring. Or obtuse and difficult. You and I know that. I don't think God wants us to hide Him in dusty old tomes that no one can fathom."

She gathered up the dishes from their coffee and toast and left him with his thoughts. When she was down the hall, he reached for his telephone. He had remembered a dear friend of his that had some influence in the publishing world. His fingers felt for the numbers as he placed the call.

III.

The small books slipped through her fingers to her lap and onto the floor.

"What have you done, Grandaddy? This is my writing, isn't it?"

"Well, you said we'd have to let God show us what to do.

So I guess you might say that He led me to make a few phone calls."

"Is this really true?"

"Yes, it is, my love.

"But who is R. Shackelford Fuqua?"

"Well, what was I going to do? Tell the publisher that this material was written by a girl with no formal training?"

"You lied to them about who wrote this?"

"You could say that, Isabella. Or you just might remember that several very famous writers have used pseudonyms. Including your beloved C. S. Lewis."

"I'm speechless!"

"Well, I'll explain while you recover your composure." He went on to tell her about her unusual copyright and contract. Only one or two people at the publishing house who were legally sworn to secrecy would know the identity of this erudite scholar named R. Stevenson Fuqua. Whatever royalties came in from Fuqua's writing would be deposited in a blind account in another city. The accounting department at the publisher would know only an account number to identify the destination of the funds. A trusted accountant in Rev. Demarco's former church had agreed to do the bookkeeping and any tax returns that might be necessary.

So, Isabella's writings continued. In an era when women had little chance to be theologians, she had a brilliant career. Because of her strong, clear style, now even the smallest Sunday School class in rural America could have a resource of rich knowledge. And the small books were not expensive.

Slowly, most church libraries and pastor's studies had a row of the colorful books on display. They were well used and studied. Dr. R. Shackleford Fuqua's reputation kept growing; however, all requests for him to have speaking engagements or give interviews were graciously declined.

The town of Little River knew only that Isabella was dedicated to the care of her grandfather. Her social life was non-existent, but she did not complain. That the Demarcos lived in relative obscurity was an accepted fact. Her parents came and went, and were relieved not to have to tend to the "old place" in Little River. When not at their condo in Florida, they traveled all over the world or visited friends they met on their travels. They knew Isabella had the home front well taken care of. Sometimes Isabella felt she hardly knew her own parents.

Isabella's life was not at all unpleasant. She made regular trips to the local stores. She participated in some of the church activities for women. Occasionally both she and her grandfather attended performances of the community orchestra held in the Gazebo near city hall. And they were always in attendance at the Lily of the Valley Community Church on Sundays. They made an interesting pair as the lovely blond girl assisted the gray haired gentleman with a white cane to their regular pew. She was careful to change as little as possible from the way things had been in his sighted days. They considered finding a seeing-eye dog for him, but as long as Isabella was available, somehow the papers were never sent in.

When Isabella was in her late thirties, her beloved Grandaddy died in his sleep. She was devastated by this loss and, for awhile, lost any joy in her life. Some time after Grandfather Demarco died, her parents persuaded her to accompany them on one of their favorite cruises: the rivers and canals of France. It was on this trip that she met and impulsively married a Frenchman of great wealth. They never had children, and the marriage ended after 8 years of less than bliss for Isabella.

In the aftermath of her failed marriage, Isabella decided to return to the only home she knew. She brought back very little from France except a generous divorce settlement, her ex-husband's tendency to swear in English, and her addiction to French coffee. She refurbished the family home on the outskirts of Little River, bought an expresso maker, and reclaimed her pew at the LOV Community Church. Her parents died within a year of one another, and after their estates were settled, Isabella found she rarely missed them. It just seemed like they'd gone on a longer trip than usual. She was grateful for their provision for her in their wills, because she was now financially secure for the rest of her life. She often thanked Jesus out loud for His beneficence.

Unbeknownst to anyone, she resumed her writing. It brought her great joy and satisfaction to know that her writing was accomplishing its purpose. She was particularly amused and pleased one day when the pastor gave her a copy of one of her own books. He suggested that she might enjoy this man's clarity of thought about theology.

Isabella knew that the theological world was slowly changing in its attitudes about the role of women in scholarly and ecclesiastical roles. She was aware that she could write and publish under her own name now; however, she enjoyed the anonymity of the pseudonym and decided not to change it.

Isabella enjoyed the pastoral calls of the new minister from the LOV Church. She and this earnest young minister developed a unique and valid friendship. It blessed her to have someone with whom she could once again communicate about subjects so close to her heart. He would come and talk energetically with her about theology and philosophy; meanwhile, he drank endless cups of her delicious latte. Once she told him that serving café latte was the one French tradition she was glad to have brought with her from France.

Sometimes he would share with her stories he had written about the LOV membership. She always delighted in clarifying the stories from her storehouse of memories about the community.

It was a blunder that introduced R. Shackleford Fuqua to Rev. Wayne. TO BE CONTINUED

Send To **Attachments**

LatimerPNG@sopac.org

Subject: Headline News

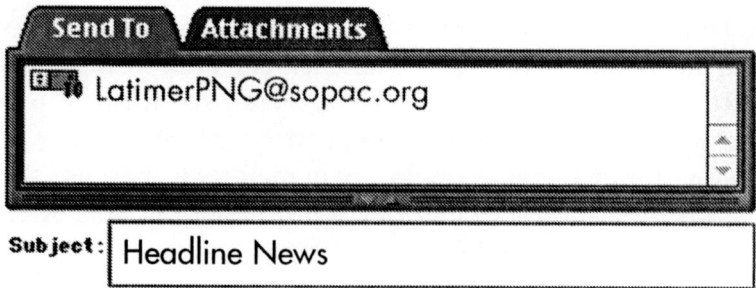

Probably you haven't lost any sleep over "the rest of the story" about Ms. Demarco. But keep reading. You'll get a kick out of how I blundered onto the "whole truth, and nothing but the truth." Anyway, sorry for the delay. I will finish up the tale about Ms. Demarco and send it over ASAP.

I shouldn't have cut the story in two, but Trudy wasn't feeling well that evening, and needed some help. She really is doing better, but has considerable pain in her lower back. The doctors are telling her that it will clear up in time, and to be patient. Nevertheless, in the interim, sometimes all that will give her any relief is hot/cold packs and a massage from her skilled personal masseuse. I never thought my illustrious career as the football team trainer would come in so handy. God's provision?

So, how are things over there? We haven't heard anything from the SoPac doc in quite awhile, so at least send us a line or two to let us know you haven't been washed out to sea on a surf board.

I can't remember if we told you that the folks were here recently for a week. They have been so concerned and worried about all of us here at LOV. It helped for them to be here, and see that we really are OK.

I haven't had a dizzy spell in quite awhile. This is definitely good news, because Stef says I can't drive until I have gone at least two weeks without any vertigo. I am like a caged bear some days, but I try to behave. I don't like being sans wheels. I think I wore Dad out running me all over town.

There really is some big news: Our small town gal turned big celebrity, Megan Gentry, is coming through in a big way for the Lily of the Valley Community Church. You remember that she is now a big shot TV anchorwoman? Since Easter, she has been determined to showcase the disaster on her program.

Megan has driven over from the big city on several occasions since the disaster. She has brought her camera crew with her a couple of times, and plans to do a special in about a month on how a community recovers from a disaster like this. She is fascinated by how the folks in Little River have gone about helping one another. Her contention is that the disaster gets the big headlines, but then the part of the story that happens in the backwash of something like our Easter Morning tragedy is rarely told.

Of course, Megan is getting lots of co-operation and encouragement around here. I'll be sure and make a video for you of the segment when it is aired. She's even been sure that my make-up is right whenever she has interviewed me. I'm very appreciative.

Stefan is some kind of proud of his twin sister and they are still very close. Sister-in-law, Ellen, has done her best to assist and accommodate Megan while this project is going on. Megan needed a liaison in the community here and Stef's wife ends up being quite a little genius at making things happen.

Now, for the really big excitement in Little River: Megan is making a major donation of her own toward funding a memorial project. She has a dream of turning the disaster site, or some property nearby, into a memorial for the victims of the disaster. She has set up a fund with her personal contribution (which is BIG) and is seeking other donors as well. She has sent out for professional bids for the memorial, but she is also encouraging citizens and schoolchildren to send in their concepts, ideas, and drawings. This really has relieved the pressure on the LOV Church family to come up with a suitable memorial. And the activity around planning the memorial has moved us all down the Healing Road a little bit farther. Praise God again!

I just opened an e-mail while I am sitting here writing to you, and it was from Raleigh saying that they are all coming home for an extended furlough. The army is sending him home on a family emergency basis. Stella really does need some consistent help, and fortunately, Raleigh could be reassigned to that base out near the airport.

He also shared a mega secret with me: they just found out that they are expecting twins. Do NOT tell a soul! They want to be here with Stella and Darcy when they make their big announcement. They all need something to lift their spirits. Darcy is turning into a very angry kid, and is acting out in major ways. I'm sure losing her father is the basis of this. She can't process her grief. Pray for all of them.

I don't think I've told you that Sam and Nora Loftis have moved back to Little River. They decided they wanted to be back "home" after the Easter tragedy. Also, the docs told Sam in no uncertain terms that he was to quit doing all that heavy work out at the lake cabin. Nora is taking over the Day Care Corral, which has been supervised by volunteers since Jenny left. Sam is going to be in charge of the LOV front office. He's such a good manager and businessman, so this is a gift right out of heaven for me.

I guess Joel is going to help them keep the cottage open out at the lake, and they'll be spending R&R time out there like old times. I think it is only a matter of time until Jill and Joel decide to tie the knot. They make a great couple. The high school kids are all interested in this romance between their coach and a quiet little classroom teacher.

Chuck, it's great to tell my secrets to you because I know you can't spread rumors over there. Just don't share the above tidbits with ANYONE. . . find a palm tree to confide in if you can't contain.

Cayla told me the other day that she misses Cousin Ashley, and we should go to Papua New Guinea for a visit sometime. You know how I spoil my kids, so I guess we'll have to work on that! I do a lot of wishful thinking these days.

Must close. The continuing saga of Ms. Demarco will follow.

Prayers and Greetings all around,
Wayne

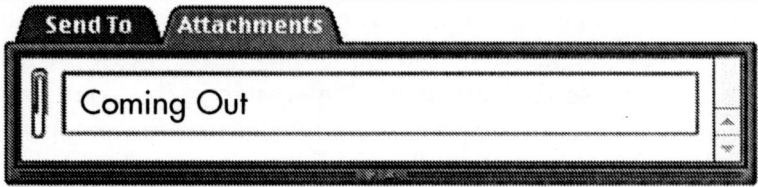

| Send To | Attachments |

| Coming Out |

COMING OUT

As Ms. Demarco busied herself replenishing his latte in the kitchen, Wayne Latimer decided to walk around her library a bit. The wealth of books on these shelves never ceased to amaze him. Even more amazing, Ms. Demarco seemed to be familiar with each one. Because she knew he would faithfully return whatever books he might borrow, he had benefited a great deal from her library. It was unusual for a small town like Little River to have such a rich resource for the ministry. Wayne felt blessed every time he left with four or five books under his arm.

Wayne was also impressed with the sophisticated computer that Ms. Demarco used like an expert. On several occasions when Wayne's limited computer skills had him totally defeated, a call to Ms. Demarco had been sufficient to walk him through the solution to his problem. Now her computer hummed behind him as he strolled by Ms. Demarco's desk and chair to see some books that interested him. When the telephone rang, she answered it in the kitchen and called to him, "Wayne, dear, I need to take this long distance call. Please make yourself at home. This call may last a few minutes."

"Go ahead, take your time," Wayne replied. For a change, he was not in a big rush to move on to his next pastoral call. As he turned back to the bookshelves, his glance fell over Isabella's desk. Several pieces of mail were stacked on top of a brown envelope from a publishing house. The computer screen glowed with a letter signed: "With kindest regards, R.

Shakleford Fuqua." The correspondence beside the computer was addressed to Fuqua and had been mailed to the publishing house by an admirer. The forwarded "fan mail" was spread out on the desk. It took but a few moments for an incredulous Wayne to figure out Ms. Demarco's ruse. He had always coveted her complete collection of Fuqua's works. Now he knew its source.

When Ms. Demarco returned after completing her phone call, Wayne wasted little time. As he set down the latte she brought him, he barged right in, "Ms. Demarco, I think we need to talk about something."

"Oh?" she replied with a rather blank stare. "Whatever do you mean?"

"Never mind," he brushed her off. "I have a question for you."

"Go ahead. What on earth is on that mind of yours, Wayne? Are you all right?"

"Let's just say a truly brilliant female wants to be a major player in theological circles, what would she have to do?"

"Well," she countered, "I suppose her chances of doing that today are better than they used to be. She'll have to attend top-notch schools. Then she must have a church or a teaching position, probably best to have the latter. And most of all, she has to be a prolific writer."

"Hmm, no church or teaching position. No hot shot degree. I think you've let down your own standards, Dr. Fuqua!"

"Well, aren't you a nosey smart-ass," she retorted without hesitation.

"Am I speaking with the famed Dr. Fuqua?" he asked with a big smile.

"You don't think Isabella would speak to you in those terms, do you?"

Thinking he might have offended her, he reached out for her hand, and said, "I honestly wasn't snooping, but as I walked behind your desk to look at your library, I saw the name at the end of your correspondence on the computer screen. I only want to compliment you, and to tell you how much I appreciate and admire what you have done. No wonder my request for Dr. Fuqua to come and lead our annual Bible Conference was politely turned down."

"You're breaking my heart," she chuckled now.

"You know, I'm still looking for a speaker for that conference. However, I think I may have found someone locally."

"And who might that be?"

"Well, this individual hasn't checked back with me yet, but I can promise you, our speaker will be one of our own LOV members."

"Who on earth are you talking about?"

"Your choice: Isabella Demarco or R. Shackleford Fuqua?"

Send To | **Attachments**

LatimerPNG@sopac.org

Subject: And The Winner Is.......

Dear Chuck,

Drrrrum Rrrrrrooooolll: YOUR DESIGN won the nod for the Easter Tragedy Memorial! Megan Gentry really likes it, thinks it's fabulous, and so does everyone else. Very creative. We were all surprised and flattered that you took the time to submit a design for our contest. Now we have to decide where to put it. Did you have any place special in mind?

Since I haven't been too good about writing you guys lately, this next e-mail will be sort of a massive "catch up" attempt. By the by, you need to do the same for us. It really helps when we know all's well over there.

What follows is about us and I guess you could call it "Family Secrets." Fasten your seat belts and don't say I didn't warn you.

Your Bro,
Wayne

Send To | Attachments

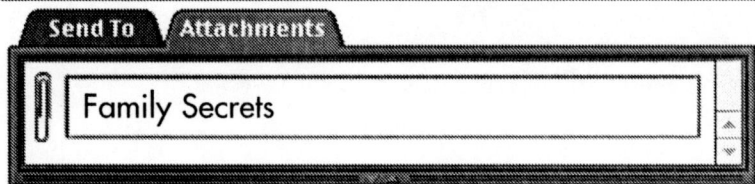

> Family Secrets

FAMILY SECRETS

The most amazing thing has happened. It is totally top secret, but I have official "clearance" from Trudy to tell you about it.

Let me back up a bit. Remember how we got Cayla? Her adoption was very quiet and private, but you recall that Sally Mix was the birth mom? At the time, I could barely remember that she had been a little ahead of us in school. I didn't even have a face to put with her name until I looked her up in our old annual

Since we were so far away in our first pastorate after seminary, the details of Cayla's adoption were never known around Little River. We adopted a baby, and that was it. Really, that was the way everyone wanted it. It was about six months after the adoption that Sally came back to Little River. I guess there was a rumor going around that she'd had a baby, but after a bit, the gossip died down. I doubt anyone from LOV knew much about her because she had dropped out on church and then moved away when she got pregnant.

All we knew was that we got a phone call from the folks about this baby that was available. Somehow Mom had heard about Sally's situation through a friend of hers at work. We told her that we were interested since we'd just had all those infertility tests done with negative results. The rest is history.

Before we took this LOV position, Trudy and I met with Sally over coffee at Lola's when we were here for our interviews. We wanted to know how she felt about us moving back to Little River ten years later, and so close to her. I mean, it was obvious we'd see each other at church and in the community. She said she would think about it and let us know.

A few days later we received a very sweet letter from her. She said she was at peace about having our family come back to Little River and to the church. However, she didn't want us to tell Cayla yet about her role as the birth mom. She thought it would be difficult for a little girl to handle that situation in her daddy's church. She even offered to move to another church if we felt like we had to tell Cayla at this time. Of course, we wanted her to stay right here with us at the LOV, so we agreed to her wishes.

As you can tell, Sally has turned into a very wise lady. She has done quite well since she moved back to Little River. She's been a regular at the LOV for years, and has served on a couple of committees. She has steadily proven herself to be a competent worker and a faithful employee in her job at the grocery. Recently, she was made the head cashier and is now practically running the store.

We decided to capitalize on her expertise, and we asked her to take over the warehouse where all the donated goods have been kept since the disaster. We really needed someone to take over the chaos at the collection site, but it had to be a volunteer because our cash is so low. Sally has been perfect for this job.

It has been a major undertaking to organize all the donations and gifts, and then to process them in a decent, responsible way. But, since Sally took over, it all runs like clockwork. She even spent her vacation running our little store. She has a major gift of organization and stewardship. We are now considering her for the church accounting job. That job is still vacant since we lost Trevor Langley in the Easter tragedy, and I really need some help with the books.

Sally has organized a great team of volunteers who have worked with her on various shifts throughout the past weeks.

So many families lost their primary breadwinner in the disaster, and the Church Store, as it has been dubbed, has been a lifesaver. People don't have to pay for the donated items that they are given, but we do keep track of what goes where.

Well, all this is to tell you that Sally has turned up with a new boyfriend: one of her top volunteers, Frank Souter. After Eva died, Frank began helping at the donation center just to have something to do in the evenings. I noticed that he was over at the Church Store quite a bit. I just chalked it up as a great way for him to heal from all his grief and hurt since the disaster. You know, he not only struggles with Eva's death and his injuries, but he had another big hit in losing Vic Dabney, his best bud since high school. I'd see him around town with a vacant look on his face, and sometimes he wouldn't even speak. But, recently I've noticed that he's beginning to come out of it a bit.

Bottom Line: Sally is a big part of why he's not so sad anymore. Sally and Frank came over to the house the other day to talk about their relationship and the possibility of their future together. Long story short, it looks like I'll probably be doing another wedding.

But they are concerned that people might think all this is too soon after Eva's death. Finally, they said they wanted me to know something that would help explain their plans for a short engagement. At this point, I was still clueless. They went on to tell me that they'd had an affair many years ago, but it fizzled. At that time, Sally was the darling of the partying crowd, and was really living on the wild side. Frank was drinking heavily, and was given to his own wild ways. They met each other one time at a party, and began to rendezvous regularly at one of the bars. It took off from there. Even though this all continued for a couple of years, they don't think Eva ever suspected.

By now, Frank and Sally have worked side by side at the Church Store for quite awhile, and they've been dating steadily for about 6 weeks. They are pretty sure that they want to begin pre-marital counseling with me. In our conversation, I could tell they've both changed and grown in the 10 years since the affair. They are different, but the same, if that makes any sense.

Of course, I'm delighted to see some joy come back into Frank's life. Now that I know about their past together, I can understand why they don't necessarily need a lot of time to get to know one another. But, don't worry, they have lots of counseling to go through with me before their wedding bells ring. I want to be sure they have a healthy relationship going. There are several big issues to address here, in case you hadn't noticed. They may need a longer time of engagement than they think if we run into problems.

But that's not the biggest news! They had me bring Trudy into the room before they told us this next part, and then afterwards we all four sat around and bawled for awhile. The big secret they wanted to share with us is this: Frank is Cayla's birth father. How come we never noticed that Cayla is the spitting feminine image of Frank Souter? Both of them were so happy and relieved to finally share this with us.

Sally told us the big reason she left town to have Cayla was that she couldn't live with the thought of breaking up a marriage. She knew Eva was bound to find out sooner or later. So she found an adoption agency out of town that would provide a place for her during her pregnancy. She never volunteered any information about the birth father, so we've never asked any questions. We do have access to some medical information on file with the adoption agency if we ever need it, but no one ever named Frank Souter as Cayla's father.

After Cayla was born, Sally eventually came back to Little River with a changed heart and a new walk with God. While she was at the maternity home, she made a clean break with her wild past. By this time, Frank and Eva were also at a whole new place with their relationship. When Sally and Frank would happen to run into each other on rare occasions or at church, they both looked the other way. After the bombing, they somehow ended up on the Church Store team, but now, 10 years later, they could handle being in the same room together. It was no problem; their lives had gone different directions for a long time. Their past connection seemed like a chapter in a book they'd read a long time ago.

Frank never knew that Sally was pregnant when she broke off their affair. He just thought she'd had enough of him, and was moving on to a bigger town to make more money. Well, one night recently while they were by themselves and bagging up groceries and supplies at the Church Store, Sally decided it seemed right to tell him what he probably ought to know. She said at first he was speechless and incredulous, and then he broke down. They just held onto each other and cried for awhile. Finally, he thanked her for all she had done for him by leaving town.

Frank went on to tell us that when Sally broke it off with him it was the turning point for him. He decided to work at being a better husband to Eva. He promised her that he would get his life straightened out and his drinking under control. He began to go to AA meetings, had an AA sponsor, and began attending church with Eva. Eva got involved with Al-Anon.

One day Frank proudly told everyone that he had become a Christian. I remember when Dad told me about Frank Souter getting his act together. He was so thrilled because everyone loves the Souters and knew they were in trouble if Frank kept going down hill.

Frank and Sally said they didn't mind if our immediate family knows about their role in our lives. We'll tell Mom and Dad the next time we are with them. I know they'll be shocked about Frank's past behavior, but happy that there are two changed lives at the end of this story. On a serious note: We think it's best to keep quiet about all this history since so many years have gone by. We've had enough to deal with at the LOV lately without hanging this story out on the grapevine right now.

Someday Cayla will know who her birthparents are, but for now, it's still under wraps. Frank told us that he has always thought Cayla is the cutest thing on wheels, and then he smiled that smile that is just like Cayla's.

Remember that Eva and Frank never had any children, so Frank is all fired up about having a family. Sally seems pretty excited too. He says he doesn't mind having a baby at his age since the baby will have such a young mother.

They have made a vow of celibacy to each other until marriage this time around. Frank says he wants to give her a bonafide honeymoon. Get this: if they keep their vow, Frank is going to reward them with the top of the line trailer from Home Designs Trailers.

They are really quite a pair, and I NEVER would have put them together in all my matchmaking schemes. You know how I love to make these things happen. Look at you and Laurie! You'd never have met if I hadn't fixed you up on that blind date.

I'm not done yet. Keep reading. I have one more secret for you, then I'll "knit up the ragged sleeve." This one is nothing short of miraculous...almost too good to be true. Remember the little girl that Stef found in the ER waiting room all by herself on Easter Sunday? Looks like she may be your niece. . . .no kidding! I'll try to make this brief and then fill in more details later.

Her name is Erika. She was visiting the church with her parents on Easter Sunday. They were travelling in the USA as tourists from Germany, and were in the proverbial wrong place at the wrong time. The family was sitting up near the front to enjoy the full benefit of an American Easter service when Donny's device went off. The parents were killed instantly, but Erika had been quietly playing with her Easter basket under a pew, and she somehow escaped without a scratch. The rescue workers heard her screams and lifted her out of the debris. They couldn't believe she was not injured, just very dusty and scared.

When Stef sent her upstairs in the hospital, she never said a word. Everyone assumed she was traumatized and would snap out of it. They kept her there over night because no one came in to claim her. You might know it was Caroline Blackwell who began to play with her in the playroom while Andrella was in the unit for observation.

Eventually, this little girl began to talk to some of the dolls and toys in the room. It sounded like she was one of those kids with her own language or something. Fortunately, one of the nurses had been stationed in Germany in the army, and she picked up on a few of Erika's phrases. When the nurse began speaking German to her, she broke out into a thousand smiles. She was even able to say her name, and to tell them how old she was with 4 fingers. She kept asking for her mother and daddy.

A rental car left in the parking lot had a lot of German papers and documents in it. When the police finally opened it, they had the missing link to the little girl's identity. They have been trying to locate family in Germany, but it looks like there are only some distant relatives who have little or no connection to Erika or her parents. They've never even met Erika. The relatives seem like decent people, they are just old and some of them are sick. They finally sent euros from Germany for the parents to be cremated and returned to Germany. They asked that the child be sent to an American orphanage. Really sad. This is a beautiful little girl in every way.

The necessary paper work was sent to the relatives, and we expect it back from Germany any day now. Of course, the immigration folks have been all over the place being sure all the "t's" are crossed and the "i's" dotted. Social services placed her out at Caroline and Will's farm for foster care, and she has been doing well out there. She has even picked up some English and plays well with the other children.

Enter your favorite pastor and wife! Caroline had heard Trudy make an off hand remark about wishing for another adoption when they were talking "girl talk" about Andrella one day. So, now we are being considered as an adoptive family for Erika. She has been coming over to our house for visits for awhile, and seems to fit right in. You should hear her go on and on in German to Bravo. He just purrs away, and lets her know that he understands every word she is saying. I think she will spend the weekend with us soon, and unless something unusual happens, we expect to have her permanently in the near future.

Remember when I asked you to pray about a third adoption for us? I never dreamed that God's answer would come through something like the LOV Easter tragedy. It has really been a healing thing to see Him give us so much "beauty for ashes."

In a way, this has put a new spin on the whole church family's recovery. Everyone at the LOV just loves this little girl. She's sort of become our "poster child." She has received more clothes and toys than any child could ever use, so a lot of her overflow goodies have been passed on to the Church Store.

Amazed by His Grace,
Wayne

LatimerPNG@sopac.org

Subject: Acts By E-mail

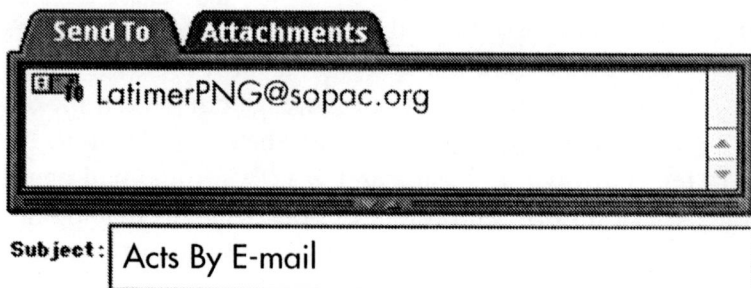

Thanks for all your well wishes about Erika. And don't you just love it when God grows people up like Frank and Sally and sets them in new places where they can honor Him? This is the best part about grace. It's fun to write about such happy events for a change. Talk about forgiveness! Talk about new beginnings!

Somewhere I read that God created people because He likes stories. I agree...like I said when we first started out here at the LOV, I feel like I'm writing new chapters of the Book of Acts all the time. I guess now our own family story has begun to blend in with the rest of the LOV stories. Maybe God likes stories because He has one of His own to tell?

I suppose you need a quick run down on the fam'? The kids are always a mess and wonderful at the same time, but you know that already. We're all pretty excited about Erika. We took her with us for a family night at the movies, and she seemed to be following the story in English just fine. Of course, Disney was a big part of that experience! Who needs words when it is all on the big screen?

Trudy has begun cooking and running the house most of the time now. She tires out soon, but these days we pretty much stay worn out anyway. We've learned the hard way that stress is very tiring. But our God is steadfast, no matter WHAT!

Love to you and yours,
Wayne, Trudy, Cayla, Joshua, and...hopefully, Erika.

P.S. I'll get some photos with the five of us on a disk soon, so check the LOV web page for them.

P.S.S. Just when things seemed pretty calm! You guessed it.......my phone rang after hours. It was Jill Sinclair in tears. Seems that she found out after school today that Joel Loftis has dumped her for a woman he met in an e-mail chat room. He's been acting strange, so she waited for him at his truck today after school, and insisted he tell her what's up.

He finally confessed what is going on. This e-mail acquaintance lives in Los Angeles and is a screenplay writer. Joel has tickets to go out there this weekend, and they'll be MARRIED in La Jolla at her producer's ocean-front mansion on Saturday night. She has two children from another marriage, and will move to Little River when this movie she is working on wraps up.

Is Joel crazy or what?

His parents aren't aware of this yet. He doesn't want to tell them until after the wedding. They will be devastated. They have always been fond of Jill, and have been so excited that she might be "the one" for Joel. (Sam was talking to me about this situation the other day over at the church office.) What makes it worse is that Joel has been accessing this Internet vixen on Sam's computer in the middle of the night since he moved back here.

Joel said that this cyber-relationship has been going on for over a year. Before moving back to Little River, he had met this gal several times on the QT out in California. It looks like Jill was just entertainment for Joel while he was alone here with time on his hands. He's shameless! Jill is so crushed, and I don't blame her. And she is some kind of angry. She certainly doesn't deserve this.

The main reason she called, Jill wanted to know if she should tell Nora and Sam what's going on. Frankly, I don't know what to advise her. I told her I needed to sleep on it and to call me during her break tomorrow. Right now, I'm not real conflicted if trusty Pastor Wayne tells the Loftises. Afterall, I didn't make any promises to Joel, and I have a big time commitment to Sam. But, I am in a quandary. Help me pray over this one, pls.

WL

Send To **Attachments**

LatimerPNG@sopac.org

Subject: Tongue Lashing

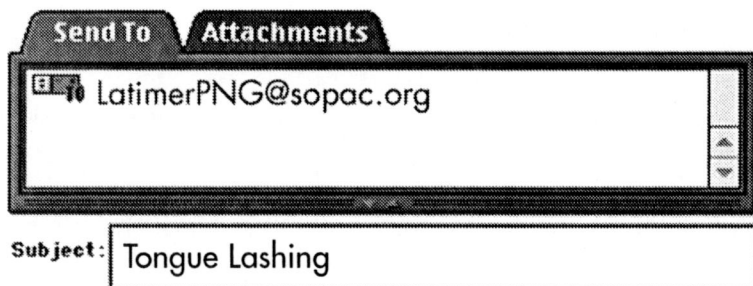

Beware:
THIS LETTER IS HAZARDOUS TO YOUR HEALTH

Well, my dear brother. You've done it up in neon this time. I am really pissed. Good thing you aren't within my reach, or I'd have you pinned to the mat by now.

What's the deal? This is a test? Right? Or maybe a joke? Say you didn't do this to me. . . . surely you jest?

I'm mortified that my masterpieces were sent warts and all to a PUBLISHER! Do I care if you knew this editor's sister back in medical school? The stories I have been e-mailing you are for you and Laurie. ONLY. That means no one else reads them. Get it? So you changed the names to protect the innocent. Thank you, God, that my brother isn't a total derelict.

And don't try to put the blame off on me because of my story about what Ms. Demarco's grandfather did with her stuff. I don't buy that excuse. You are perfectly capable of dreaming up this debacle on your own. I am not guilty of initiating this crime in any way. Give me a break. I'm a victim of sibling abuse at the highest level, and I need a therapist. I'm definitely sending you the bill.

Chuck, the Main Thing is: These Are Not My Stories. They belong to God and the people who are following Him who just happen to belong to my flock. I'm not the author, I'm not the think tank, and I don't sit around and dream these up. I'm only a part of my own story that shows up occasionally in my e-mails.

It just occurred to me: I guess Luke had a similar problem with his friend, Theophilus, when he was writing his stories down in the first century. After all, somehow, Luke's stories found their way into the Bible. Old Theophilus obviously told someone. Thus we are blessed with the Book of Luke and the Acts of the Apostles. You and Mr. T are partners in crime. Am I comforted by this information? NOT! Have you noticed, these stories aren't exactly about Jesus and Paul Inc.?

Since I have vented and told you off, I feel a lot better. So I will now share with you what happened early this a.m. You guessed it, your publisher guy called me. (I read your e-mail confessional about this just before I went to bed, so I at least had a little warning.) It seems that he "likes my stories," and wants to know more about me and about my church. I told him in no uncertain terms that I could lose my job if some of this information hits the streets. He says this problem pops up all the time. The editors work diligently on it to be sure that no one's true identity is revealed.

This is very scary, Brother!

All right....so I'm vain enough to be flattered. But I am still radically griped. I am relishing this opportunity to honestly haul you over the coals. I await your apology.

Your sainted baby brother,
Wayne

P.S. How many autographed copies shall I reserve for you?

Printed in the United States
6844